W9-CAX-293

1. Elevator Entrance
2. Lobby
3. Faculty Offices
4. Cafeteria
5. Auditorium
6. Courtyard
7. Mailroom
8. Classrooms
9. Gymnasium
10. Training Hall
11. Library
12. Dorms
13. Garden
14. Armory
15. Train Station
16. Vault

LOST IN THE MUSHROOM MAZE

WRITTEN BY **BEN COSTA &
JAMES PARKS**

ILLUSTRATED BY **BEN COSTA**

ALADDIN
New York   London   Toronto   Sydney   New Delhi

For Kiev and Heidi

ALADDIN

An imprint of Simon & Schuster Children's Publishing Division
1230 Avenue of the Americas, New York, New York 10020
First Aladdin hardcover edition May 2022
Copyright © 2022 by Ben Costa and James Parks
All rights reserved, including the right of reproduction in whole or in part in any form.
ALADDIN and related logo are registered trademarks of Simon & Schuster, Inc.
For information about special discounts for bulk purchases, please contact Simon & Schuster Special Sales at 1-866-506-1949 or business@simonandschuster.com.
The Simon & Schuster Speakers Bureau can bring authors to your live event.
For more information or to book an event contact the Simon & Schuster Speakers Bureau at 1-866-248-3049 or visit our website at www.simonspeakers.com.
Cover designed by Dan Potash
Interior designed by Mike Rosamilia
The illustrations for this book were rendered digitally.
The text of this book was set in Oneleigh Pro.
Manufactured in the United States of America 0422 FFG
10 9 8 7 6 5 4 3 2 1
Library of Congress Cataloging-in-Publication Data
Names: Costa, Ben, 1984- author, illustrator. | Parks, James, author.
Title: Dungeoneer adventures 1 : lost in the mushroom maze /
written by Ben Costa and James Parks ; illustrated by Ben Costa. Description: New York :
Aladdin, [2022] | Series: Dungeoneer Adventures ; book 1 | Audience: Ages 8 to 12. |
Summary: Coop Cooperson is the only human kid at the Dungeoneer Academy,
a school for the future explorers of the Land of Eem, a place full of monsters, mazes, and danger;
together he and his teammates (Oggie the bugbear, Daz, a boggart, and Mindy, an imp) are
having their survival skills and understanding of the Dungeoneer's Code tested in a treacherous
obstacle course—but many more challenges lie ahead, and so far Coop is failing miserably
(as everyone points out), just like a previous human student, Dorian Ryder.
Identifiers: LCCN 2021020950 (print) | LCCN 2021020951 (ebook) |
ISBN 9781665910699 (hc) | ISBN 9781665910705 (ebook)
Subjects: LCSH: Schools—Juvenile fiction. | Explorers—Juvenile fiction. | Labyrinths—Juvenile fiction. |
Bullying—Juvenile fiction. | Friendship—Juvenile fiction. | CYAC: Adventure and
adventurers—Fiction. | Schools—Fiction. | Explorers—Fiction. | Labyrinths—Fiction. |
Bullying—Fiction. | Friendship—Fiction. | LCGFT: Adventure fiction. | Novels.
Classification: LCC PZ7.1.C6743 Lo 2022 (print) | LCC PZ7.1.C6743 (ebook) |
DDC 813.6 [Fic]—dc23
LC record available at https://lccn.loc.gov/2021020950
LC ebook record available at https://lccn.loc.gov/2021020951

~ INTRODUCTION ~

MY NAME'S COOP COOPERSON, AND I'M THE only human at Dungeoneer Academy. *What's Dungeoneer Academy?* you ask. A school for kids to learn the ropes of being an explorer in the Land of Eem, a place full of different species of people, as well as monsters, mazes, mayhem, and maybe even a little magic! Cool, right?

Every class at Dungeoneer Academy is divided into four teams, each with its own color: red, blue, yellow, and green. I'm on the Green Team!

Together my friends and I go on amazing adventures to discover forgotten ruins and find lost treasures . . . all while encountering strange creatures and characters (some nice, some not so nice).

This book you're reading now is basically my personal adventure journal. And my best friend, Oggie, draws all the pictures. So if you're up for a wild ride, strap in! Because at Dungeoneer Academy . . . adventure is our favorite subject.

CHAPTER

1

THAT'S IT, I'M DEAD MEAT. I KNOW, I KNOW.
The story literally just started, but I am TOAST.
In fact, we *all* are.

Need proof?

Check out the gnarly creature chasing me and my friends.

That thing's called a ramgore.

Extremely grumpy. And do you see those horns? Trust me, you don't want to be on the business end of those horns.

That's me, Coop—front and center. Coop Cooperson. Yes, my name is *really* Coop Cooperson. And if you didn't already know, you're reading my adventures. I keep a journal

of everything that happens to me. Mainly because I'm the only human kid *ever* at Dungeoneer Academy.

My best friend, Oggie—he draws all the pictures. That's him on the right. The tall bugbear, eyes wide and panting hard. He's basically, like, the best artist in the whole school.

Next to Oggie is Mindy. She's an imp. And right now she's struggling to keep up because of that giant backpack of hers. Weighs her down like an anchor. Who wears a backpack that huge, filled with that much random stuff? Mindy, that's who. She says it's because a dungeoneer needs to be prepared for anything. Which is true. But one thing I've learned over and over again in my short time here at Dungeoneer Academy . . . you also need to be prepared to run for your life!

Luckily, Daz is there to give Mindy a hand as we leap for the slimy rock wall in front of us. Daz is a boggart, and easily the most awesome of our team. She's smart, fast, skilled . . . and, well, kinda cute.

Wait a minute—I can't be thinking about cute girls at a time like this! Get your head in the game, Coop! Your future at Dungeoneer Academy is riding on this. All of our futures are!

I clamber up the slimy surface of the wall, and almost slip to my doom. But my hands find a firm grip, and I barely pull myself out of harm's way as the ramgore slams its mighty horns into the wall with a **THUD!**

Whew! That was close. But there's no time to rest. We run full speed ahead into the next hallway, and out of nowhere this green, stinky gas pours from a vent in the stone walls. Ick! A gas trap! It smells like an ogre ate a trash salad sandwich and burped in my face. We've got to keep moving.

"Wait!" Mindy yells.

CLICK!

I accidentally step on a pressure-plate! Something sharp and pointy whizzes by my head.

CLICK! WHIZZ! WHOOSH!

We dash forward, not even watching where we step! Gouts of flame blast from jets in the floor and ceiling! We weave through them, the fire so hot it burns my nostrils.

All of a sudden a pendulum blade swings toward us from the darkness above.

"Duck!" yells Oggie.

We dive out of the way. Well, everyone except Mindy. She hits the floor, and her humongous backpack tumbles onto her head. The pendulum narrowly misses slicing her in two.

"Mindy!" I scream.

"I'm fine!" she says, muffled under her backpack.

WHOOSH!

GO ON WITHOUT ME!

The pendulum sways back and forth above her like an old tire swing. Well, an old, razor-sharp, murderous tire swing.

"Just stay down!" I reply. She'll be fine if she doesn't move. But we've got to press on. Time is against us.

We charge forward, and next thing I know, Oggie sticks out his big furry arm to stop me from plunging down into a pit.

"Whoa. Thanks, pal!" I say.

"Don't mention it," says Oggie. He sighs.

I hate this part . . .

"Just follow my lead." I take a step back and jump to the first platform in front of us.

Daz leaps right behind me as I leap to the second platform, and Oggie follows her.

Now, I should probably explain something about Oggie.

Oggie is superstrong, and like I said before, he's a great artist. Oh, and of course he's the best friend anyone could ever ask for. But Oggie . . . well, he's kinda clumsy. He says he's still growing into his body, and sometimes his big old feet can't keep up with his brain.

And that's exactly what happens as he leaps from one platform to the next. Oggie's feet go all wonky, and he spins out of control like a dizzy ballerina.

BAM! Oggie accidentally bumps into Daz, and she loses her footing too. I turn around, but there's nothing I can do. They both go tumbling into the murky water below with a **SPLASH!**

"Oggie!" Daz yells as her head bobs up from the water. She's clearly frustrated.

"Sorry, Daz." Oggie is soaking wet and looks about a hundred pounds thinner.

"Whatever," Daz mutters under her breath. She turns my direction as I bound to the other side of the chasm.

And then it's all up to me.

But just when I think there's time to take a deep breath and get my bearings, I hear the sound of grinding stone so loud that it rattles my bones. I glance behind me and see a giant boulder rolling down a ramp from above. My legs feel like jelly, but if I don't move now, I'll be pancake batter!

The boulder slams on the ground where I was just standing a second earlier, and the whole dungeon shakes like an earthquake. Small rocks pelt me from the ceiling, and I can't help but scream. I dart through the dark tunnel as the boulder barrels behind me just a few feet away.

Then I see it. The glowing pink gem. It's sitting on a golden pedestal at the other end of a pit. By the look of things, I'll need to swing on a ropy vine hanging from the ceiling to get to the other side of the pit. I don't have a moment to think.

But right before I jump, I make the dumb, dumb, DUMB decision to look down. Staring back at me from the darkness below is a giant spider. I stop in my tracks. My knees start shaking. I can see its ooey, gooey mandibles glistening in the dark. Did I mention I hate spiders? Like, *really* hate them?

So, this is where I actually die. I know I said I was toast earlier, but I really think I'm going to have to end it here, folks. I never should have enrolled in Dungeoneer Academy. No Junior Dungeoneer Badge is worth this! I mean, I certainly

10

didn't expect that I would die in my first semester! Maybe I'm just not cut out for this stuff.

As I contemplate my mortality, I hear the faint voices of my friends echoing through the dungeon. "Come on, Coop! You can do it!" they say. "You're our last chance!" And suddenly I'm filled with a little bit of hope.

At least enough to leap out of the way of the rolling boulder before it flattens me!

Only trouble is, I didn't have a running start. I barely grab hold of the vine and cling for dear life. But without any momentum? I can't swing to the other side!

"Come on!" I wiggle on the vine like a worm on a hook. I'll never get the gem now.

Falling into a dark pit is bad enough, but worse than that . . . I'm about to be spider food. The giant spider's fangs foam and froth as it inches toward me. My sweaty hands slip, and I slide down the vine.

CHAPTER

2

SO THERE I AM DANGLING TEN FEET ABOVE
the slathering jaws of a humongous spider, when suddenly the lights switch on. No, I don't mean I get
some bright idea about how I'll defeat the eight-legged beast
and somersault heroically across the pit. . . . I literally mean
the lights. Everything turns bright, and time is up.

FWEEEEEEEET!

It's the unmistakable sound of Coach Quag's whistle,
followed by his gruff voice. "All right, recruits! The Trial
Gauntlet is over! Get him down from there!"

Coach Quag shakes his head in disappointment as a

COACH QUAG, GAUNTLET INSTRUCTOR

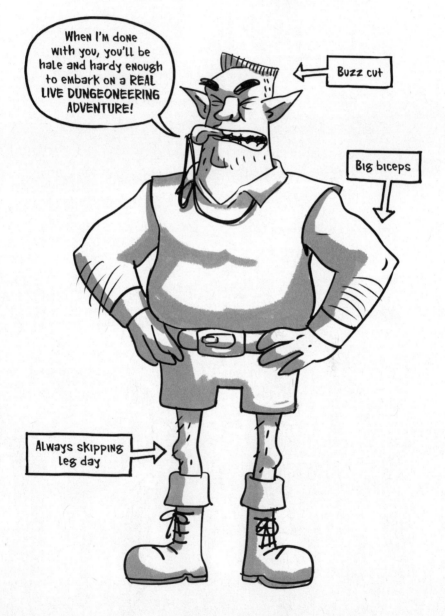

mechanical platform slowly extends across the pit below my feet. I let go of the vine and drop to solid ground, my hands sore from clenching so long.

Below me, the giant spider skitters up the walls of the pit to Coach Quag.

"Mr. Fang," says Coach Quag to the spider. "Thank you for your time. You can resume your duties in the library."

Okay, so I have a confession to make. Maybe the giant spider wasn't really about to eat me. But he sure *looked* scary! You try swinging across a pit with a menacing, ten-foot spider looking up at you. Oh, and while you're at it, let this sink in. Dungeoneer Academy has a *giant inkpot spider* for a librarian. And his name is Mr. Fang.

A shudder goes down my spine as the monstrously huge Mr. Fang glares at me. I see my horrified reflection quadrupled in his black eyes. I gulp. Spiders *really* creep me out.

Coach Quag returns his attention to me. "Pitiful! Just pitiful! I've seen some poor performances in the Gauntlet before, but that was just . . . BAD."

By now you're probably wondering what in the world Coach Quag means by "the Gauntlet." The Trial Gauntlet is our version of a pop quiz. It's basically a tricked-out obstacle course that pushes your physical and mental skills to the limit. Coach Quag says it'll whip us into shape and turn us into dungeoneers for real.

What exactly is a dungeoneer? you ask. Well, for me to really answer that question, you'll need a bit of a history lesson on the Land of Eem. That's where we live. It's a big continent full of monsters, mazes, mayhem, and maybe even a little magic, if you know where to look!

So sit back and let me take you on a journey into the past. It all started a long time ago. Like, a really, really long time ago, back when there were enchanted forests, magical wizards, fire-breathing dragons, and whole cities made of gold. Oh, and there were lots of humans everywhere. But then something really bad happened, and everything changed.

My mom called it the Cataclysm, which I think is just a fancy word for "HUGE DISASTER." Professor Clementine told us that there was a big war and the Land of Eem became cursed. The cities of gold crumbled, the enchanted forests faded away, and I guess all the wizards and dragons disappeared too. And the humans, well, there're not so many of us anymore. All of our history was lost, for the most part. Buried under a thousand years of dirt. But every once in a while, something special turns up, like an artifact or a shiny piece of treasure! And that's where dungeoneers come in.

We dungeoneers are professional explorers (well, I'm not a professional yet, of course) who dedicate our lives to the discovery of the world that used to be. We're part archaeologists and part adventurers, who embark on quests to find lost cities, historical relics, strange new creatures—and piece together the mysteries of the forgotten world.

Dungeoneer Academy itself is located underground in a place called the Underlands. Which is basically exactly what it sounds like. A whole world beneath our feet where caves and tunnels all intertwine like a big maze. A place where giant underground cities carved out of rock bustle with all sorts of species of people going about their daily lives. It's pretty cool.

To be perfectly honest, though, living underground as the only human at the school has been a bit of an adjustment. I'm used to fresh air, tall grass, and babbling rivers, but I guess if you replace fresh air with musty egg farts, tall grass with jagged rocks, and babbling rivers with burbling slime, it's close enough. Besides, if you really want to be a dungeoneer, then Dungeoneer Academy is the place to be.

It's pretty much this amazing adventure school where we study subjects like Dungeons and Mazes, Combat and Tactics,

Creatures and Critters, Riddles and Runes, Myths and Legends, and of course, Swords and Sorcery! Plus there are six grade levels at Dungeoneer Academy: recruit, junior, scout, cadet, apprentice, and explorer. Me? I'm a lowly recruit. But by the time we graduate, we'll all be full-fledged dungeoneers. Ever since I was little, I've dreamed of being one. Discovering lost civilizations, delving into mysterious caves, finding buried treasure.

But I digress! It looks like story time is over, because Coach Quag is NOT looking happy. You can tell by the vein pulsing in his forehead. I've seen it so many times, I decided I should give it a name. Everyone, meet Moe the pulsing vein.

"That was just awful! Worst Trial Gauntlet I've seen in years. Face it, Cooperson. You're a screwup."

"A screwup?" (I think that's a little harsh, wouldn't you say?)

Coach Quag growls like a manticore. "You hesitated! Real dungeoneers don't hesitate. When a dungeoneer hesitates, it could be their last mistake. After all, fortune doesn't favor the hesitater. Fortune favors the bold!"

"Sorry, Coach." My voice is so quiet, I can barely hear myself.

"Sorry doesn't cut it, recruit. I mean, you spoiled a perfectly good opportunity to leap heroically across a pit, for goodness' sake! And what did you do instead?"

By now the rest of the class has piled into the room. The usual suspects. Blue Team, Yellow Team, and Red Team, all wearing their color-coded neckerchiefs. UGH. Red Team. They're the worst.

Zeek and Axel from Red Team

"Um . . . I froze?" I reply to Coach Quag, my voice warbling in my throat.

"That's right, you froze!" he barks back. "And to make matters worse . . ."

Uh-oh. Coach is really mad now. I think Moe is about to burst once and for all as Coach Quag pounds his clipboard. But then he calms himself down with a loud sigh, and Moe retreats from view for a moment.

"To make matters worse, you left your party behind!" Coach grimaces and points behind me to Oggie, Mindy, and Daz, who are all looking the worse for wear. "Not that *they* fared any better . . .

"That's two tenets of the Dungeoneer's Code you messed up in a single run, Cooperson! Do you even *remember* the Dungeoneer's Code?"

Do I remember it? Of course I remember it! The Dungeoneer's Code is the ultimate standard of what it means to be a dungeoneer. It defines the dos and don'ts of dungeon exploration and exemplifies the dungeoneer spirit of adventure. There are ten tenets of the Code. The first three tenets are what we call the Big Three. They're kinda like our goals and objectives while out in the field. The next seven tenets help guide us when things get a little hairy.

~ THE DUNGEONEER'S CODE ~

1. Discover new life and lost civilizations.
2. Explore uncharted places.
3. Unearth and preserve our collective history.
4. Expect the unexpected.
5. Never split the party.
6. Always check for traps.
7. Every problem has a solution.
8. Every dungeon has a secret door.
9. Cooler heads prevail.
10. Fortune favors the bold.

"So which two tenets did you utterly and miserably neglect?" Coach leans forward mere inches from my face. That vein. It's like Moe is trying to communicate with me. I can't stop staring.

WELL?!

Uh . . . "Never split the party," and "Fortune favors the bold."

"That's right! Now take a good look, recruits. What did we learn today?" Coach Quag folds his arms and furrows his eyebrows as he addresses the rest of the students. They just stare at me like I'm some kind of weirdo. I mean, sure, I'm the only human kid at Dungeoneer Academy. Everyone else is a boggart, goblin, bugbear, imp, dratch, shrym, or welkin.

But I'm not a *weirdo*, am I?

Then it happens. Zeek raises his hand.

25

Zeek and Axel are the bullies of Red Team. Zeek's the leader and Axel's the muscle. They've both been on my case ever since I enrolled in Dungeoneer Academy, but Zeek's the meanest.

Zeek steps forward, grinning with that mouth full of sharp teeth. "You hear that, everyone? Spiders! What a wimp!" Everyone laughs.

Great. Just great. Now *everyone* knows I'm afraid of spiders. Literally my second-worst nightmare, behind, you know, actual spiders.

"Don't listen to that jerk," Oggie says, putting a giant furry hand on my shoulder.

"Thanks, big guy." I can always count on Oggie to have my back.

OGGIE TWINKELBARK, HERO OF THE REALM

Oggram Twinkelbark, "Oggie" for short, is my best friend. I told you that already, right? Anyway, he comes from a long line of mighty bugbear warriors. In fact, Oggie's dad is the CWO (chief warrior officer) of their village—bugbears that dwell in the eastern mountains and spend their free time wrestling ettins and smashing boulders with their foreheads.

Oggie's not much for boulder head-bashing or ettin wrestling, though. He may look big and tough, but Oggie's a big softie. Like I said, Oggie is an artist. When he's not drawing the cool pictures in this here adventure diary, you can usually find him reading the comics in *Dungeoneer Magazine*, or chowing down on orch rinds. Maybe both at the same time!

THE REAL OGGIE

"Besides, as far as spiders go, Mr. Fang isn't so bad," Oggie says, trying his best to make me feel better. "Not all inkpot spiders are dangerous, you know."

"'Not all are dangerous' implies that SOME are still dangerous," I reply. "You do realize that?"

Oggie smiles. "You're hopeless."

At that moment, Coach Quag blows his whistle to quiet everyone down. "Now listen up, recruits. Today was just the Trial Gauntlet. And a good thing too! Because if you fail the FINAL Gauntlet, not only will you NEVER receive your Junior Dungeoneer Badge, but . . . you'll be expelled."

The whole class gasps.

This can't be for real. Expelled?

"Being a dungeoneer isn't some happy-go-lucky walk in the park! Being a dungeoneer is serious business. Life-and-death! You slip on a rock? You're dead! Fall into a pit full of spikes? You're dead. Swallowed by a gwarglebeast?

Arnie Popplemoose, a squirrely shrym on Blue Team, gulps. "You're dead?"

"Wrong! You'll be roasted alive in its belly for three days! Then you'll be dead," barks Coach Quag. "So listen up, and listen up good! If you can't even pass the rinky-dink Trial Gauntlet, you've got no place bein' out in the field on a real-life quest. It would just be irresponsible of me to let that happen. Better to just send ya home back to your mommies and daddies or whoever the heck your legal guardians happen to be, okay?

"I'm looking at you, Green Team." Coach Quag gives us the evil eye. Oggie, Mindy, Daz, and me. But mostly me. At least that's what I'm thinking. I'm the one who let everyone down.

"All right, recruits. Class dismissed!" Coach Quag hollers

and blows his whistle. "Lunchtime! Go get yourselves some protein! And practice your lunges!"

As most of the other students pile out of the Trial Gauntlet chamber, I just stand there and stare down at the giant spider-web in the pit. Mr. Fang is gone, but I'm still shaken up.

"Looks like spiders are the least of your troubles, eh, Coop?" Zeek narrows his eyes, and that smug, sharp-toothed grin widens. "I see expulsion in your future. Just like Dorian Ryder."

"Dorian who?"

"You really don't know?" Zeek scoffs. "Dorian Ryder was the first human at Dungeoneer Academy, and the WORST student the school has ever seen."

That is, uNtil YOU came aLong aNd took the cake!

ha ha!

Dorian Ryder? Another *human*? I had no idea. I wonder why no one ever told me.

I know I shouldn't pay Zeek any mind, but for some reason his words stick with me like gutter-snail glue. What if he's right? What if I really don't belong at Dungeoneer Academy?

"Shut up, Zeek."

Zeek and I both turn and see Daz standing with her hand on her hip.

DAZ, GREEN TEAM MVP

Cool hair

Cute ears

Not impressed by Zeek

Pet snagbunny named Peaches

Dazmina Delonia Dyn. But don't call her that to her face. Just "Daz." She's basically the coolest person I know. Daz is like a born dungeoneer. The MVP of Green Team, for sure. And check this out. Daz is also great with animals. That's, like, her thing. She has a pet.

Only thing is, Daz pretty much keeps to herself. Which makes it hard to really get to know her. Which I totally want to do because, well . . . I kind of like her. Like, *like* like her. You know what I mean. What's not to like, right? Wait, I'm not blushing, am I? Please say I'm not blushing! Worst nightmare number three . . . Daz finds out I *like* like her. Now, that would be embarrassing.

Zeek shuffles his feet. Even he doesn't want to mess with Daz. Gosh, she just keeps getting cooler.

"Psh! Whatever," scoffs Zeek. "Later, losers. And, Coop? Better watch out for spiders when you go beddy-bye!" Zeek and Axel laugh like hyenas as they walk off.

Before I can say thanks to her, Daz has disappeared too.

"Hey, Coop! Over here!" Oggie hollers, waving to me. "You coming or what? It's mystery casserole day!"

My stomach churns at the thought. "Yuck," I groan. "I don't know how you eat that stuff, buddy. You know, I bet the secret ingredient is ogre snot. . . ."

BLORF
THE ORCH COOK

CHAPTER

3

*S*LOP!

Two mounds of steaming, hot goo crowd my plate. The dreaded mystery casserole. But here's the real mystery. . . . Am I supposed to *eat* this stuff? It looks more like something you'd find smooshed under a troll's foot than anything you'd put in your mouth. I stare at Blorf, the cook, in disbelief.

If there's one thing I miss most about home—you know, besides my family—it's my mom's cooking. What I wouldn't give for a nice steak, some mashed potatoes, and a side of corn on the cob. Heck, I'd even happily devour all that spinach my mom used to beg me to eat.

Then, without so much as an oink, Blorf slops something else onto my plate. Something alive and wriggling. I audibly shriek, but Oggie oohs with delight.

"You've outdone yourself today, Blorf," he exclaims.

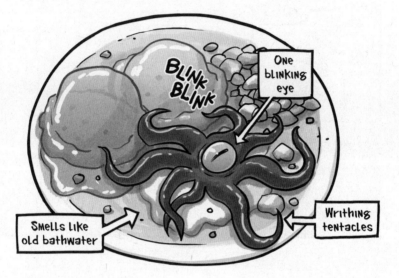

See, Oggie doesn't seem to have any problem with the food here. In fact, he loves it. Oggie is like my family's pet goat, Walter, back home. One time Walter went on an eating spree and scarfed down one of my dad's boots, a plank of wood, and an empty bottle of rascal cider. The only bad thing that happened to him was he got a nasty case of the burps.

With our lunch trays in tow, Oggie and I move to find a seat at one of the cafeteria tables. It's crowded, but we usually have no trouble finding a table for ourselves. . . .

See what I mean? That seems to be how it goes around here for me. I try to take it in stride, but on days like today, well, it's hard not to be bothered.

"They think I'm a monster, Oggie."

"They just don't know you, Coop," says Oggie. "If they knew you, there'd be a line out the door to sit next to you at lunch."

"Yeah, right. They don't even wanna know me."

"Who doesn't want to know you?" says a high-pitched voice. We look up to see Mindy's familiar, spectacled face across the table. She sets her humongous backpack down beside her on the bench. It's so big, it's like another person is sitting with us.

"Being well liked is overrated," Mindy says matter-of-factly. "It's better to just focus on your studies and shut out all that extra noise. I didn't enroll at Dungeoneer Academy to win any sort of popularity contest."

Then, without missing a beat, she looks us both dead in the eyes.

"If you guys had just stopped for a second, I could have deduced where the pressure-plates were hidden in the dungeon floor. I have a whole system!"

Mindy Darkenheimer is a genius. Well, technically her full first name is "Mindisnarglfarfen." And she says imps don't usually have *last* names because they're summoned into existence by hex magic. I'm not really sure what that means, but Mindy was adopted by the Darkenheimers when she was just a baby. So "Mindy Darkenheimer" it is!

MINDY DARKENHEIMER, GIRL GENIUS

She grew up somewhere far to the north in the mountains, and all she ever had to do to entertain herself was read her parents' dusty old tomes on geography and ancient lore. Mindy is pretty much the smartest person I've ever met, and that's including all the teachers at Dungeoneer Academy. Trouble is, she can be a bit of a know-it-all sometimes, which gets on the teachers' nerves.

But I like Mindy. She's awesome, and always prepared. Always. And we actually have a lot in common. We both have to work a little harder than everyone else to stay afloat at Dungeoneer Academy, and neither of us is ready to leave just yet.

"Mindy," says Oggie slyly. "A little suggestion. Maybe if you crammed less stuff into your backpack, you wouldn't be such a slowpoke."

"Everything in here is absolutely essential," Mindy replies.

Then Mindy starts pulling all these glass tubes and flasks from her backpack. It looks like she's assembling some sort of chemistry experiment at the table.

"Uh . . . what's all *that* for?" I ask.

Without looking up at me, she dumps the food from her tray into a funnel. "I'm making the food *edible*," she says with a smirk.

We all watch the mystery casserole ooze through the tubes, mixing with some sort of liquid that Mindy has prepared. Unfortunately, when it comes out the other end of the tube, it almost looks less appetizing. Just a pile of brown goop.

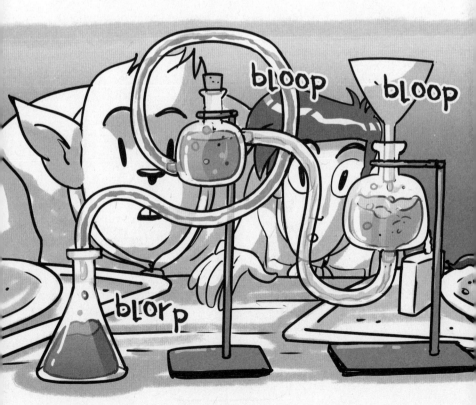

"Go ahead, Coop," Mindy offers. "Try it."

"I guess it can't be any worse than it already was, right?"

Mmm! Tastes like CHOCOLATE PUDDING!

"Wow, this is great, Mindy!" I exclaim. "I'm gonna need this gizmo for every meal. I bet you could make a small fortune if you sold this to the other kids."

Mindy looks content as she eats a spoonful. "That's what Daz said too."

My heart races just at the mention of her name.

"Where is Daz anyway?" I ask, trying to be nonchalant. "I, uh . . . I never got a chance to thank her for sticking up for me."

"Oh, you know how she is," Mindy says. "She's off by herself somewhere."

It's true. Even though she and Mindy are bunkmates, Daz is a bit of a loner. Odds are she's in the campus garden or playing with her pet snagbunny, Peaches.

"That's fine by me," says Oggie. "I don't need her breathing down my neck all the time. It's bad enough that my dad is always on my case." Oggie deepens his voice and does an impression of his father: "You're better than that, Oggie! You'll never amount to anything if you don't shape up!"

"Hey, at least your dad seems to care, Oggie," Mindy says. "Daz's parents are too busy to pay her any attention. She hasn't heard from them since school started."

"Really? Is she okay?" I ask as I lean in. I guess Oggie senses my interest.

Coop . . . do you have, like, a crush on Daz or something?

WHAT?!

"Interesting hypothesis, Oggie!" Mindy says, raising an inquisitive eyebrow over her glasses. "Well, do you, Coop?"

"No! Of course I do!" Did I just say "do"? Coop, you goober! "Don't! I mean 'don't'!"

SPLAT!

Something wet and slimy hits me hard in the side of the face. A blob of mystery casserole. I wipe it from my eyes and spot Zeek across the cafeteria. He's holding a spoon, which he presumably used to launch said mystery casserole like a catapult. A skeevy, smug grin is plastered on his face.

"That's it," I say under my breath. "I've had just about enough of this bully."

But Mindy grabs me by the arm before I can leave the table.

"Coop—stop!" she implores. "He's not worth it. We're already on thin ice as it is. You think getting into a fight with Zeek Ghoulihan will make that any better?

"No," she says, answering her own question. "We've just got to hunker down and study. Eyes on the prize, Coop."

She's right, of course. I can't jeopardize my time at Dungeoneer Academy just because of some annoying wiseguy like Zeek. Besides, everyone else on Green Team is counting on me too. I can't let my friends down.

But something's been nagging at me ever since Zeek said it.

"Can I ask you two something? Who . . . who was Dorian Ryder?"

Mindy's face scrunches. "Why do you want to know about him?"

"Zeek said he was the first human to go to Dungeoneer Academy before he got expelled. And that he was the worst student ever." I wipe some casserole off my face and scan the room. "Is that how people see *me*?"

"Just because you're both human doesn't mean you're the same person, Coop," Mindy replies. "From what I know, you couldn't be more different. Besides, Dorian Ryder was expelled a long time ago."

"But Zeek said—"

"Forget about Zeek," Oggie chimes in. "He's just a bully."

"I know, but . . . I mean, come on. Worst student EVER?"

"First of all, that's not the story I heard," Mindy says, leaning in with a whisper. "I heard Dorian Ryder was just a recruit.

45

But he was an incredible student. Gifted, you know? Everyone expected him to be the best dungeoneer ever, until . . ."

"Until what?"

"Ryder was apparently pretty brash. Didn't like to follow the rules, and cheated during the Final Gauntlet."

"Cheated?" My brow furrows.

"Worse, actually. All he cared about was winning. Ryder *sabotaged* the other teams, and they got hurt pretty bad. Headmaster Munchowzen expelled him on the spot."

"Whoa. . . . I never heard that part," Oggie gasps.

"You know about this too?" I ask.

"Well, kinda. I thought it was just a story." Oggie hands me a napkin to wipe the rest of the casserole off my face. "Here, you missed a spot."

The bell rings. Lunchtime's over.

"Off to class," Mindy says cheerily. "Dungeoneering 101!"

CHAPTER

4

ONE OF THE BEST THINGS ABOUT Dungeoneer Academy is Professor Clementine's class. She teaches Dungeoneering 101, which is basically an introduction to what it takes to be a dungeoneer.

But mostly she just tells us stories. Don't get me wrong, though—they are really GREAT stories. Adrenaline-packed tales about discovering the lost ruins of ancient civilizations, making first contact with creatures that have a hundred eyeballs, even escaping the clutches of an evil riddle master that trapped her in his riddle maze! The only story she's never told us is how she lost her eye and her leg. But no one ever asks, because that would just be rude. Although, my money's on the evil riddle master.

47

PROFESSOR CLEMENTINE, DUNGEONEERING 101

"Dungeoneering is important work," Professor Clementine exclaims with passion in her voice. "Without dungeoneers, the untold histories of Eem would lie dormant in the forgotten recesses of the world. It is our job to find those keys to the past. After all, this is our history—*all* of ours. Whether you're a boggart, a dratch, a goblin, a human, or anything in between. If we can understand the past, we can better plan for the future together."

Professor Clementine scribbles furiously on her chalkboard. "And there is so much to be learned! Science, culture, lost technology, and some even believe . . . magic!"

"Pfft, I don't believe in magic," mutters Zeek.

Professor Clementine spins abruptly on her heel, eye aflame. "As dungeoneers we must be open to new ideas, new experiences, new perceptions of the people and world around us. Only by understanding ourselves and one another can we truly appreciate and cherish our treasured heritage."

As Professor Clementine continues her lecture on the importance of dungeoneering, I just can't stop myself from daydreaming about the *Adventures of Green Team in the Underlands*! My pencil scrawls wildly as I imagine myself holding a crackling torch and delving into a deep, drippy cavern to find the lost treasures of the Beast with a Hundred Eyes. . . .

"Mr. Cooperson?" Professor Clementine stands over my desk, leering at me with her one good eye. "Are you listening? What are the first three tenets of the Dungeoneer's Code?"

I snap out of my daze and put down my pencil. It might have looked like I was taking notes, but really I was writing in my adventure journal. I can't help it!

I sit up straight, as attentive as I've ever been. I can't help but recite the Dungeoneer's Code with reverence. Just think about it! For generations these guidelines have been followed by some of the greatest adventurers ever. And every time I recite the tenets, I get a feeling of pride. But not everyone treats the Code that way. In fact, from behind me I hear the familiar bored groans of Zeek and Axel.

"That is correct, Mr. Cooperson. Well done. But do pay more attention. . . ." Professor Clementine's eye widens as she glares down at my adventure book.

"Yup. Just taking my notes here," I say nervously. "See? Lots of notes."

She raises an eyebrow and turns away. Phew!

"Now, class. Today's lesson is about what we dungeoneers refer to as *party composition*. Preparation for the Final Gauntlet shouldn't be taken lightly, you know." Professor Clementine raps her knuckles on her wooden leg. "And party composition is the first step in assuring that you and your companions are operating as a well-oiled dungeoneering team!

"First off, who can tell me what a *party* is?"

"What, like a birthday party?" says Oggie. "You know, presents and balloons. Maybe some cake. Dang, I love cake."

"No, Mr. Twinkelbark. Not a birthday party. An adventuring party. 'Party' is another word for 'TEAM'!" Professor Clementine snaps to attention. "And team is everything!

"And proper party COMPOSITION is how we build our teams so that the members complement each other's skills. Why do you think it's important to complement each other's skills?"

Professor Clementine scans the room. "Mr. Eggtooth?"

"Um. What?" Axel scoffs like he's too cool for school. "Sorry, teach. You talkin' to me?"

Then Daz speaks up confidently. "Good party composition is important so that the team works together better. Everyone complements each other's strengths that way."

"Correct, Miss Dyn!" Professor Clementine claps her hands. "You all have special talents individually. But no one is perfect by themselves. Combine your talents, help each other, and your teams will be sure to succeed."

Professor Clementine grabs a stick of chalk and starts furiously scribbling on the chalkboard. "At Dungeoneer Academy we categorize our talents into four primary statistics to measure a team's success!"

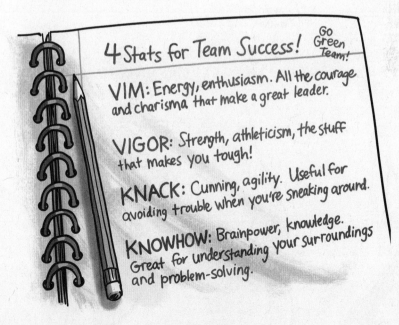

4 Stats for Team Success! Go Green Team!

VIM: Energy, enthusiasm. All the courage and charisma that make a great leader.

VIGOR: Strength, athleticism, the stuff that makes you tough!

KNACK: Cunning, agility. Useful for avoiding trouble when you're sneaking around.

KNOWHOW: Brainpower, knowledge. Great for understanding your surroundings and problem-solving.

Putting down the chalk, Professor Clementine spins around with gusto. "When your team's talents combine in the right way, when balance and harmony are achieved . . . nothing will deter you from running the Final Gauntlet and earning your Junior Dungeoneer Badges."

Professor Clementine sits down, almost out of breath. "Questions?"

The room is quiet. You can tell that everyone is thinking about their own talents. How they each fit on their teams. After all, the Final Gauntlet is do-or-die. And frankly, I'd rather not die. But what have I ever been good at? I like to think I'm pretty good at writing stories, but how's that gonna help me in the Final Gauntlet?

As these thoughts roll around in my head, I stare at Daz sitting at her desk.

She's practically sparkling as she writes in her notebook. I can't believe she stood up to Zeek like it was nothing! That's a lot of vim, if you ask me. And how many other kids in school can do backflips through fire traps? Yeah, I've seen her do that too. It was awesome. Gosh, that's a lot of vigor, right? And don't even get me started on her knack and know-how. She's literally got a snagbunny named Peaches for a pet. And did I mention she passes all her classes with perfect scores?

Sigh. Maybe Professor Clementine was wrong. Some people are just perfect. Daz could be her own team. . . .

"Spider! A spider! Get it off! Get it off!" I flail my arms and leap onto my desk like a frightened cricket. My books and papers fall to the floor with a clatter, and everyone turns to look at me with their mouths agape like I'm some sort of alien.

The hairy, black tangle of legs flies from my hand and skitters across the floor.

"Mr. Cooperson!" shouts Professor Clementine. "What is the meaning of this?"

"S-spider," I whimper. "There was—it was—" Ever since coming to Dungeoneer Academy, I've developed a bad habit of stammering when I'm nervous. Maybe Coach Quag was right—I hesitate too much. That, or I just can't seem to catch a break! The whole class snickers and rolls their eyes.

"Sit back down right this instant. Didn't I tell you to pay attention?"

"It's just a spider, Coop. . . ." Daz picks it up casually and stares at me.

Zeek belts out a sinister laugh. "Nice one, DORIAN. Way to show the class just how COWARDLY humans are!"

"Don't call me Dorian!"

"Ha ha! You want me to write a letter to your mommy? You ready to go home yet?"

"Zeek Barfolamule Ghoulihan!" Professor Clementine growls. "If I didn't know any better, I'd be inclined to think you had something to do with this."

"What? It's just a spider." Zeek smiles smugly, laces his fingers together, and leans back in his chair.

Suddenly time is running extra slowly. Everyone's voices come out like tuba sounds, while the whole class gawks at me as if I'm some weirdo loser. Even Oggie is giving me a funny look. I don't know what to do. I can't cry. That would make things a million times worse. I'm clammy all over, queasy, even. I mean, I've always felt kind of out of place at Dungeoneer Academy. But right now? Now I feel like I don't belong at all. Maybe Zeek's right. Maybe I should just go home.

BRRRRRRNNNNG!

Mercifully the bell rings! Maybe I can catch a break after all.

"Class dismissed!" Professor Clementine yells over the clamor of scraping desks and chairs.

Within seconds the room is half-empty. I jump to my feet, but Professor Clementine stops me in my tracks. "Except for you, Mr. Cooperson."

Great! Stupid Zeek. I'm innocent, I tell you! Innocent!

The classroom is now completely empty except for me and Professor Clementine. "Take a seat, Mr. Cooperson," she says in an even voice, and slides her stool closer to my desk.

"First of all," I say, starting into my defense with my hand over my heart, "I was totally paying attention, and if it weren't for Zeek and his—"

Professor Clementine cuts me off with a smile and a wave of her hand. "You're not in trouble," she says. "Actually, I see that you have a lot of potential."

"Really?"

"Really."

"But?" There's always a but, right? Has to be. I know it's coming.

Professor Clementine smiles at me slyly. "No buts. You just have a lot of potential. I know it must be hard being the only human at the academy. Not to mention living underground and experiencing some strange new normals.

"The truth is, you know your stuff, Cooperson. Not very many students admire the Dungeoneer's Code like you. But you need to focus. Be more attentive. I encourage you to write in that journal of yours. Just not in class."

"Sure thing, Professor Clementine." I stuff my adventure journal into my bag and stand up. "Wait, can I ask you a question?"

"What is it?"

"Did you know Dorian Ryder?"

Professor Clementine's expression turns uneasy. "Yes, I did. Mr. Ryder was a gifted and troubled student."

"Did he really hurt all those kids?" I ask.

"Unfortunately, he made some choices that hurt many people." Professor Clementine folds her arms and stares into the distance. "All he cared about were his own selfish desires. It didn't matter to him who got hurt along the way. Ultimately, Dorian was expelled from the academy for abandoning the Dungeoneer's Code."

"What exactly did he do?"

"That doesn't matter. Besides, you have other things to worry about." Professor Clementine gives me a funny smile. "Oh, and just one last thing, Cooperson," she continues, walking me to the door. "You have a great shot at earning your Junior Dungeoneer Badge. The Final Gauntlet might be daunting, but if you work together as a team and remember the Dungeoneer's Code, you'll be sure to succeed. You're a natural leader. Follow your instincts. Green Team's lucky to have you."

Natural leader? Me? It's impossible to hide the smile on my face. Professor Clementine really is the best. There's a new spring in my step, and I can't help but bolt out of the classroom and run down the hall. I gotta tell my family about this!

CHAPTER 5

OKAY, LET ME TELL YOU ABOUT MY FAMILY.
I have fifteen brothers and sisters. Yep, you read
that right. Fifteen.

There's Kip, Chip, Flip, Candy, Tandy, Randy, Kate, Kat, Kit, Hoop, Hilda, Mike, Mick, Mary, and Donovan. Oh, and don't forget Walter, our pet goat.

We don't have much, but we certainly have each other. Lots and lots of each other. My brothers and sisters and I used to spend all our time running around the bayou near our house, catching frogs and fireflies, playing riverball, and taking our boat out to fish.

As you can imagine, I didn't have much privacy at home. Didn't even know the meaning of the word. When you have fifteen brothers and sisters, getting a moment alone is next to impossible, even in the bathroom.

I'm not too sure what my parents were thinking, having so many kids, but hey, *this* is my normal.

Oh, and, uh . . . this is my house.

My family lives in a giant barrel.

Go ahead, you can laugh. I give you permission.

I know now that it's kinda weird, but growing up, I just assumed everyone lived in a giant barrel.

See, my dad comes from a long line of coopers. Hence the last name "Cooperson."

And if you didn't know, coopers are crafters. We make all kinds of stuff out of wood, like barrels and buckets and tubs and horse troughs. Even coffins. (Luckily, my family doesn't live in a giant coffin. That'd be creepy, wouldn't it?)

MY DAD

Wears the same overalls every day

Barrel chest

Always has tools

Anyway, it's the family business. And because I'm the oldest kid in the family, it's basically my destiny to follow in the footsteps of every Cooperson who came before me.

But here's what I'm getting at. . . .

That's not me. That's not what I want to do when I grow up. I don't want to make barrels and buckets and tubs and horse troughs all day. And I definitely don't want to make coffins.

I want *adventure*. I want mystery. I want to search for old relics! And make first contact with amazing creatures! I want to discover ancient ruins that hold secrets to the past! You know, like all the stuff you'd read about in *Dungeoneer Magazine*.

As a little kid I devoured stories about the legendary Shane Shandar and his harrowing expeditions into the Shimmering Shar! Shandar is a real hero and always seems to know what to do in a sticky situation. And you can bet he never hesitates in a tense moment.

I dreamed of accompanying Shane Shandar on his adventures, even writing stories of my own. But that's all it was . . . a dream.

Then one day I received a letter in the mail. . . .

My jaw just about hit the floor when I read those words.

Me? Accepted into Dungeoneer Academy? I hadn't even sent in an application!

I mean, I had *written* one, but I'd never submitted it.

See, a while back there was a contest in *Dungeoneer Magazine*.

🔥 **DUNGEONEER ACADEMY** 🔥

Do you long for ADVENTURE?
Do you dream of exploring LOST WORLDS?

NOW'S YOUR CHANCE!

Write a personal essay about why YOU should be our next Dungeoneer Recruit!

Dungeoneer Academy is the premier school for future explorers and adventurers in the Land of Eem. Learn from the best, most experienced professors, embark on amazing quests, and live by the Dungeoneer's Code!

All essays will be read and judged by Dungeoneer Academy founder Headmaster Geddy Vel Munchowzen himself!

Attend the very same institution where world famous dungeoneer Shane Shandar graduated!

Write today! Send your essay to:

Dungeoneer Academy
c/o Headmaster Munchowzen
1530 40th Tunnel Way
Underlands 'neath UTBF

Name _____

Address _____

☐ I want to be a Dungeoneer Recruit!

Dungeoneer Academy!
Where adventure is our favorite subject!

So I wrote my essay. Spent a long time on it too. But I never sent it in because I never thought in a *million* years they'd accept me—Coop Cooperson—some poor kid from the backwaters of the River Country. Who could imagine me at Dungeoneer Academy?

Also . . . I didn't know how my parents would react.

Would they be mad that I don't want to become a cooper when I grow up?

But guess what? . . . Turns out my mom found my application and sent it in for me! Can you believe that? Aren't moms the best?

Incredible mom strength

MY MOM

At least two kids hanging on her at all times

Basically the best mom in the world

My whole family couldn't be more excited for me.

Well, that's not *exactly* true. My dad—he's not so keen on the idea of me being off at some faraway school, learning how to be an "adventure-seeker," as he calls it. He'd rather have me at home with him in the workshop, learning how to be a proper cooper. Times have been a bit tough lately. River Country's not the richest place in the Mucklands, after all. And with sixteen mouths to feed? It can be hard to get by.

Luckily, my mom was able to convince my dad that this could be a big opportunity. I could be the first Cooperson to get a degree, and really help the family out. I guess it's an honor, but going off on my own is scary too. Sometimes the world feels like it's all riding on me. . . . But hey, I'm at Dungeoneer Academy! How can I complain?

Every week my family sends letters, updating me about life at home.

Dear Coop,
Glad to hear you're doing well and classes are going smoothly! Your brothers and sisters loved Oggie's drawings you sent over. And Daz sounds like a lovely girl. You tell that Coach Quag to lighten up a bit. He sounds like a stick in the mud.
　　Now for the weekly roundup.
Everything's going fine here on the bayou. Daddy's been working down in the shop

every day, but as you know, it can be slow this time of year. He wishes you were here to help, of course, but knows you're working hard in school.

Kip, Chip, and Flip all made the riverball team. Candy, Tandy, and Randy joined the tadpole choir, and Kate won the spelling bee. Kit and Kat both lost their front teeth, and Hoop and Hilda are learning how to read your old *Dungeoneer Magazines*. Mike, Mick, and Mary are climbing on everything these days. And Donovan said his first word: "Coop!" How about that?

I show him your picture every day.

We all miss you so much, Coop!

Love,
Mom, Dad, Kip, Chip, Flip, Candy, Tandy, Randy, Kate, Kat, Kit, Hoop, Hilda, Mike, Mick, Mary, Donovan, and Walter!

I send letters back every week, telling them all about how things are going here at school. Well, mostly. I've been kinda leaving out all the bad stuff about maybe being expelled, and getting bullied by Zeek. I know I shouldn't be keeping secrets, but I just don't want to worry or disappoint them.

My mom always says they're doing fine, but I know times are tough with money. And there are a lot of mouths to feed in the Cooperson household.

I don't want to be too greedy, but if I ever find treasure one day on a dungeoneering adventure . . . well, it would help out my family a ton. Mom and Dad could use a bit of treasure.

Because the truth is . . . my family . . . however hard up they've been without me, they gave me a chance to fulfill my dreams. I mean, come on. I'm at a school that teaches you how to be an adventurer! What's better than that? I need to work hard, apply myself, and focus. Because getting expelled and letting them down? I can't let that happen.

CHAPTER

6

HEY, CUT IT OUT!"
Zeek wrenches my neck into a headlock, stuffing
my face into the crook of his sweaty armpit. It stinks
like fish butts and cabbage. I didn't even see him coming.

I try to wriggle free, but no dice. As far as headlocks go . . .
and I've been in a few . . . Zeek's is like a vise. Those arms
might be lanky, but they're STRONG.

"Come on, Zeek. Quit clowning around! Let me go!"
I shift my weight and almost twist free, but Zeek's grip just
tightens.

"Um, let me think about that. A clown asking *me* to stop
clowning around?" Zeek mocks. "Yeah, gonna have to be a
hard no on that one, POOPERSON."

I can't help but marvel at how lazy Zeek's insult is. I mean, he couldn't have surprised me just a little?

"Let him go, Zeek." Oggie steps up, as big as a house. Oggie will make short work of Zeek for sure. Go for it, Oggie!

"Back off, Tiny," snarls Axel.

Oggie shrugs. "Tiny? I'm six three!"

"Yeah? Well, then you're a six-foot-three-inch twerp." Axel flexes his blue, scaly muscles and pounds a clawed fist into his palm. "Come on. . . . Wanna wrestle?"

"Um, no," Oggie squeaks as Axel lifts him off the ground.

"You hear that, Zeek?" Axel hisses as he slams Oggie into the locker. "Oggie doesn't wanna wrestle!"

Zeek chuckles with delight. "Good luck winning your

Junior Dungeoneer Badge with that guy, POOPERSON. Who ever heard of a bugbear that wouldn't wrestle?"

So here I am huffing Zeek's fishy, boiled-cabbage armpit, and Oggie is pinned up by Axel like a wall decoration. To add to the embarrassment, Blue Team and Yellow Team are forming a crowd to watch the show. Let's just say this situation could have gone a tad bit better.

"I guess Twinkletoes here is too busy doodling to put up much of a fight." Axel grabs Oggie's sketch pad and tosses it onto the floor.

"That's Twinkelbark!" cries Oggie.

"Twinkletoes!" Zeek laughs with wicked glee. "I thought 'POOPERSON' was a dumb name. But 'Twinkletoes' takes the cake!"

That's it. Say what you will about me, but nobody messes with my best friend. With a swift tug and a nimble roll, I break free of Zeek's grip and spring to my feet. Digging in my heels, I draw my finger like a sword and poke Zeek in the chest.

"Back off," I growl with confidence.

But Zeek just stands there and lets out a squealing, high-pitched laugh that sounds like a balloon losing air.

"You back off!" Zeek pushes me so hard, I trip and land on my tailbone with a thud. Sprawled on the ground, I watch Zeek and Axel laugh. Then the crowd gets quiet. Nobody steps in.

Nobody but Daz, that is.

Daz pushes through the crowd and squares off with Zeek and Axel. Her eyebrows are furrowed, and her hands are balled up into fists. "You want to bully someone?"

Suddenly Zeek's not so confident and glances at Axel for backup.

"You okay, Coop?" Mindy scurries over and helps me up.

"Well?" Daz outlines her challenge. "Go ahead and bully me, Zeek."

Zeek freezes, gulps, then steps toward Daz sheepishly. He's nervous, for sure, but I can see a kind of thoughtful calculation in his eyes. "Whatever," he finally says. "At least I'm not a loner. At least I have friends."

Daz doesn't flinch. "Oh yeah? Well, at least I'm not a baby."

Zeek cackles. "Baby? What's that supposed to mean?"

"You heard me. In fact, I've got it on good authority that you love your pacifier." Daz betrays a wry smile, but her eyes are still fierce.

"W-what? What are you talking about? I don't have a pacifier! Binkies are for babies!" Zeek's voice falters, and again he glances back at Axel, who just shrugs.

Suddenly Daz springs into action. In a blur of movement she leaps into the air, reaches out with her hands, and proceeds to flip over Zeek.

After snatching something from Zeek's backpack, Daz lands in a graceful pose, hair whooshing behind her. "Well, then, this must make you a baby," Daz says, holding up a pink baby pacifier and smiling.

"What? That's not mine!" Zeek cries out. "That's not mine!"

Everyone in the hallway starts laughing, voices chiming in that Zeek's a baby.

"Shut up! Stop laughing!" Zeek fumes, his green skin turning red. A vein pops out on *his* head, so huge that it would give Coach Quag's Moe a run for its money.

Axel's scaly throat swells up, and then the beastly dratch lets out a guttural guffaw. Tears stream down his cheeks. Axel is laughing so hard, he buckles over.

Zeek scowls at his friend, and shoves him! "Shut up, Axel!"

"Nice work, Daz!" Oggie slaps her on the back with a big hairy paw.

"Yeah, way to go!" Mindy beams and claps her hands.

I'm just about to thank Daz when suddenly Arnie Popplemoose barrels into the hallway.

"Big news!" gasps Arnie, panting like a dog and drenched in sweat. "Big, big news!"

"Slow down, Arnie," I say. "What is it?"

"Headmaster Munchowzen!" Arnie's eyes are bulging out of his head. "Announcing the Final Gauntlet location! In the auditorium! Everyone, hurry!"

And just like that the crowd of students erupts and everyone bolts to the auditorium. Finding out where the Final Gauntlet is being held is a really big deal. Once we know where we're being tested, we can start to figure out what kind of wacky obstacles to be prepared for.

"Let's do this, team!" Mindy says, adjusting her glasses. "It's GO time."

"You said it, Mindy!" Oggie snatches up his sketch pad and follows Mindy out the door.

Daz twirls the pink pacifier in her hand.

"Hey, Daz! Wait a second." I stop her before she bolts after Mindy. "So, how'd you find out Zeek uses a pacifier?"

"Oh, he doesn't."

"Wait, what?" My jaw drops so far to the floor, I can practically taste gym socks.

"It actually belongs to Peaches, my snagbunny. Helps her sleep." Daz pops the pacifier into her pocket.

"Wow," I laugh. "Good move."

"Yeah, well . . . I don't like bullies." Despite having really shown Zeek who's boss, Daz doesn't seem that thrilled. I can't put my finger on it exactly, but it's like she's almost sad.

"Hey, that s-stuff he said about you being a loner," I stutter. "That's not true. I've . . . I've always considered you a friend."

"Thanks. You too, Coop." Daz stops by the door and turns around with a smile. "You coming or what?"

Without another word, I follow Daz out the door, and we dash down the hallway as fast as we can. The whole school is buzzing. Final Gauntlet, here we come!

CHAPTER

7

S ETTLE DOWN, SETTLE DOWN!" HEADMASTER Munchowzen bellows from the auditorium stage. "Settle down now, children!"

The entire class finally hushes up, and the headmaster scans the room with squinted eyes.

Headmaster Munchowzen is impossibly old and wizened. He kinda looks like a raisin if it had a long nose and a big white mustache. The headmaster always wears the same clothes too: an old, musty green coat, festooned with colorful medals and badges from his storied dungeoneering days.

Some of the kids, like Zeek and Axel, make fun of him behind his back because he can't hear all that well. But they're just jerks. Not many people would guess it today, but Headmaster Munchowzen is one of the greatest dungeoneers that ever lived. He's actually the founder of Dungeoneer Academy, and legend has it, he even created the Dungeoneer's Code! Now, that's pretty epic if you ask me.

HEADMASTER GEDDY VEL MUNCHOWZEN, FOUNDER OF DUNGEONEER ACADEMY

"We are gathered here today to reveal this year's location of the Final Gauntlet!" the headmaster continues. "The last test of your first semester here at Dungeoneer Academy. So without further ado . . ."

I look next to me down the row at Oggie, Mindy, and Daz, all listening in rapt attention. I can hardly contain my excitement.

"This year's Final Gauntlet will be held in . . ." Headmaster Munchowzen is clearly enjoying the anticipation. "The FUNGAL JUNGLE!"

At that, a huge banner flaps and unfurls onstage behind the headmaster, a massive tapestry depicting a sprawling mushroom wilderness.

the fungal jungle

The crowd erupts, and all the kids start yakking and chattering about what this means:

"The Fungal Jungle!"

"Wow!"

"Can you believe it?"

"This is going to be great!"

To be honest, though . . . I have no idea what the Fungal Jungle even is.

"Settle down, now!" the headmaster exclaims, and everyone clams up again. "The Fungal Jungle is the largest expanse of untamed flora and fauna in the Underlands, which makes it the perfect place to construct a Gauntlet.

"As you know, each year a brand-new Final Gauntlet is designed for our students to triumph over. And this year the designer is none other than our librarian, Mr. Fang."

My heart drops in my chest like a sack of doorknobs. *Mr. Fang?!* You've gotta be kidding me! Great! Just great! There are totally gonna be spiders, aren't there? Tons and tons of horrible, nasty spiders!

I'm so doomed.

Mr. Fang skitters onto the stage and stops next to Headmaster Munchowzen. Everyone's clapping, but I've broken out into a cold sweat and my hands are gripping my seat tight.

"Mr. Fang," the headmaster says, addressing my worst nightmare, "do you have any words for the students?"

Yeesh! Talk about giving me the creeps!

"There's gonna be so many spiders," I squeak.

"You think?" muses Oggie. "Nah, that's too obvious. I bet Mr. Fang will go with something like snakes. Don't spore cobras live in the Fungal Jungle, Mindy?"

I hear Mindy *Eek!* at the thought of spore cobras. If I hate spiders, Mindy hates snakes just as much. Okay, maybe not *just* as much (how could that even be possible?), but still, she's no fan of snakes.

"Blech! Why'd you have to remind me?" Mindy says. "Spore cobras are extremely deadly. Did you know they spit acidic spores into the face of their prey before they bite? Now, that's scary!"

"You two are overreacting," says Daz, raising an unimpressed eyebrow. "There's nothing wrong with snakes and spiders. I have a pet tarantula *and* a singe viper at home. I mean, you have to handle them with care . . . but they're cute!"

"Sure, Daz," I say. "Not my idea of cute."

"Oh yeah, then what is your 'idea of cute'?"

"You" comes to mind. But I'm glad I don't say *that* out loud.

"Pay attention, children! Eyes up here," Headmaster Munchowzen shouts. "First thing tomorrow morning, you will all embark on a three-hour sputter-train journey into the belly of the Fungal Jungle. There you will be escorted to the hidden location of the Final Gauntlet. Of course, Professor Clementine, Coach Quag, Mr. Fang, and I will be accompanying you and grading your performance in the Gauntlet."

The headmaster clears his throat, and a serious look sweeps across his wrinkled face. "You will be tested on your skills, yes, but also on your conduct. Safety in our time-honored trade is paramount. Which is why we hold these important trials. After all, dungeoneering is not for everyone. We are explorers! Adventurers! Archaeologists! Preservers of history and protectors of our shared heritage. Only the most diligent and dedicated among you will advance to graduation. You must study hard and keep fit!

"Conquering the Final Gauntlet will be no easy task. It will take courage, discipline, teamwork. Perhaps even a bit of luck. But most important, I urge each and every one of you to live by the Dungeoneer's Code. To uphold it in all that you do. If you live by the tenets of the Code . . . well, you won't need luck." He pauses, and his eyes sweep the room.

"Now go," he says. "Make sure to get a good night's rest. Tomorrow is a very important day. . . ."

It's impossible to tell, but suddenly it feels like Headmaster Munchowzen is staring directly at me. Like his squinty eyes are seeing right into my soul. **GULP!**

CHAPTER

8

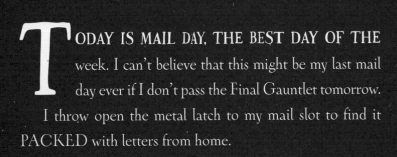

TODAY IS MAIL DAY, THE BEST DAY OF THE week. I can't believe that this might be my last mail day ever if I don't pass the Final Gauntlet tomorrow.

I throw open the metal latch to my mail slot to find it PACKED with letters from home.

"Wow. It's gonna take me all night to read these!" I exclaim, swimming through the pile of letters from all my brothers and sisters. I'm so preoccupied, stuffing my backpack with mail, I almost miss Daz on the far side of the mail room.

"Hey, Daz! Check out this haul! I can barely lift them all! What'd you get?"

Daz closes her mail slot and turns the key, without a word.

"Um, so, how's it going?" I ask, a little sheepishly. "Any news from home?"

Daz must not have heard me. She doesn't turn around or anything, just walks straight out of the mail room. Kind of odd, but Daz does like to keep to herself sometimes.

Just then Mindy walks in and offers me a wave.

"Hey, Mindy."

"Hi, Coop!" She drops her giant backpack and flutters up to her mailbox with her little imp wings.

"Mindy, can I ask you something?"

"Sure, what's up?" Mindy replies, thumbing through a couple of letters.

"It's about Daz. Does she seem a little off to you?"

"Of course she does. It's mail day."

"What do you mean?" I ask, genuinely confused. Mail day is the best. Mail day is when you finally get to hear from your family and friends back home. Don't get me wrong, Dungeoneer Academy is great, but it's still a boarding school. I get homesick all the time.

"Daz doesn't get any mail. Like I said, her parents are sort of . . . never around."

"Oh." It's all I can think to say, because honestly, I feel like such a jerk. There I was just moments ago rolling around in a pile of letters, when Daz didn't get any. "Maybe I should go apologize. I didn't realize I was being so inconsiderate."

Mindy flutters back down to the ground and puts her enormous backpack on. "I don't know. Maybe just give her some space. And don't put on such a big show next time."

I think about what Mindy said as I take the long way back to the dormitory. I like taking the long way because it goes through the Academy Garden, which is always peaceful this time of day. Plus it's nice to enjoy some quiet alone time—something I never have back home. That, and if I take the garden route, I can avoid walking past the library, where Mr. Fang is no doubt lurking.

But I can't stop feeling like I put my foot in my mouth with Daz. She seemed pretty upset back there. It's so easy to get wrapped up in my own life and my own problems, I can forget what other people are going through sometimes. But Daz isn't just my classmate. She's my friend. And friends look out for each other. Never split the party, right?

When I finally get back to our dorm room, I see Oggie hunched over and painting up a storm.

"Whoa! Is that what I think it is?" I drop my pack and get on my knees to examine Oggie's newest project.

"Yup. My dragon shield."

"This is legitimately the best thing I've ever seen in my life." I'm dumbfounded. Oggie has really outdone himself! "How long did it take to make this? I mean, when did you even have time?!"

Oggie licks the tip of his paintbrush and dabs on an orange
glob to brighten up the dragon's flames. "Built it in Professor
Shrewman's shop class. Been working on it awhile, but today
I decided to take it home and put the finishing touches on the
dragon's scales and flames. You know, to represent the Green
Team. What with the Final Gauntlet coming up and all . . ."

Oggie spits on his thumb and wipes off a smudge of blue paint. "I'm not sure it's done, though."

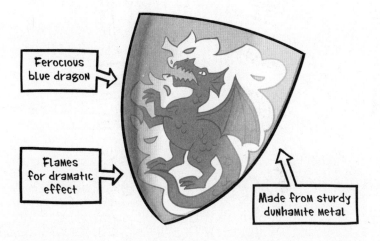

Ferocious blue dragon

Flames for dramatic effect

Made from sturdy dunhamite metal

"Um, Oggie. This shield is astounding," I say. "Like I haven't said it already, but you're a really talented artist, man."

"I don't know." Oggie tosses his paintbrush aside and sits on the desk chair. "You're the only one who thinks so."

"That's not true," I reply, sitting on the bed across from Oggie.

"Oh yeah?" Oggie pulls a letter from his pocket. "It's from my dad."

"What does it say?"

"Usual stuff. Good old Chief Twinkelbark is looking forward to my certain victory in the Final Gauntlet. Can't wait to tell the rest of the village about my feats of strength and warrior prowess." Oggie hands me the letter absentmindedly. "Read the postscript."

P.S. Drawings are nice and all! Just remember, drawings don't bend bars, lift gates, or bash doors down! Be strong, wrestle hard, and eat a lot! After all, you're a Twinkelbark!

"I don't know, Og. Your dad said your drawings were nice." I hand the letter back to Oggie.

"'Nice and all.' Not the same thing. Besides, I know he doesn't care." Oggie puffs out his chest and barks mockingly, "I'm a Twinkelbark! I'm just a big, bad bugbear." He stands up, beats his chest, and stomps around the room. "I'm as tough as a titan and don't take any guff! Psh! My dad just wants me to be exactly like him. But I'm not. I have my own interests, you know? Just because I'm big doesn't mean I'm cut out to be some warrior guy like he is." Oggie picks up his shield and slides it slowly under the bed.

"Come on, Oggie," I say, sliding the shield back out again. "I get what you're saying, but maybe you just need to talk to him a bit. Believe me, I can relate. My dad still wants me to become a cooper when I grow up."

"Coop Cooperson the cooper?" Oggie asks with a puzzled look.

"Well, yeah. Coopers make barrels and horse troughs and stuff. And since I'm literally the SON of coopers, my dad has certain expectations, you know? But parents can surprise you sometimes. Despite their reservations, they helped me get here to fulfill my dream. Now I've got a shot at being a dungeoneer. We all do."

"Yeah, I guess," Oggie says. "You're right about one thing, though." He lifts up his big, furry head and smiles. "We do have a shot at becoming dungeoneers."

"You heard me. We have a Final Gauntlet to prepare for!" Mindy grabs me by the hand, trying to tug me out of the room.

"What? Where are we going?" I ask.

"We need to learn as much as we can about the Fungal Jungle before tomorrow. We need to know what we're up against. Dungeoneer's Code number four! Expect the unexpected."

Mindy snatches Oggie's dragon shield off the floor. "Here!" she exclaims, and gives it to Oggie.

"My shield? What for?" Oggie asks.

"Might need it," she says curtly.

"What? Why?" Oggie spins in place, confused. "The paint's not even dry."

"Hold on." I stop Mindy as she starts off down the hall. "Where are you taking us? It's almost time for bed."

"We're going to the library."

"Whoa. Mindy. The library's closed," I say. "No one's allowed inside at night!"

Also, Mr. Fang is in the library! I do everything in my power to avoid the library! Seriously, I've never even checked out a book. Oggie does it for me.

"Correction! The library's FORBIDDEN at night," Mindy replies. "So, no one to bother us. Now hurry up. Daz is meeting us there."

"But—but, Mindy!" I stammer. This can't be happening.

Mindy grins slyly. "Come on. What are you . . . scared?"

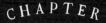

CHAPTER

*C*REEEAAAAK.

Mindy opens the massive library door, and I wince, half expecting Mr. Fang to be waiting right there, ready to nab us. But no, it's just pitch-black darkness. We inch forward. The coast is clear . . . for now.

"I d-don't like this," I stutter as we shuffle down the aisles of towering shelves, all stacked with old books, tomes, and scrolls.

Daz yawns. "This better be worth missing sleep, Mindy. I could be snuggling with Peaches right now."

"Who would want to snuggle a snagbunny?" Oggie snickers. "That's like sleeping next to a chain saw, with all those sharp teeth."

"Peaches is cute!" Daz retorts.

"Pipe down, you two," I say, scanning the ceiling above, unable to see anything but wispy cobwebs in the darkness. "Let's just make this quiet and quick. Emphasis on 'quick'!"

"Quit being such a worrywart, Coop," Mindy chides. She leads us down a dark aisle filled with books that haven't been checked out in ages. Mindy wipes a layer of dust off a huge purple book with ragged edges. *"Legends of the Great Fungal Jungle,"* she whispers.

Perfect.

We all tiptoe to one of the study tables and pore over the book, hoping to learn anything useful about the Fungal Jungle. Something to give us a leg up for the Final Gauntlet so we're not caught off guard.

"The Fungal Jungle is the largest wilderness biome in all of the Underlands," Mindy reads aloud. "It is composed of lush, colorful fungi forests inhabited by a wide variety of strange plant life and creatures that have yet to be fully catalogued. Many believe life in this peculiar region is interconnected and grows from the very spores of the tallest toadstool trees.

"At the center of the Fungal Jungle lies the mysterious

Mushroom Maze...a natural, impossible-to-navigate labyrinth of rare and poisonous mushrooms."

"Sounds like the perfect place for an obstacle course full of death traps, if you ask me," I say. "Note to self: don't eat any mushrooms."

"Whoa, look at that," Daz blurts as Mindy flips through the pages. We all stare at a horrifying beast illustrated on the page.

Fig. 108. The Gwarglebeast

"Now, don't even try to say *that* thing is cute," snorts Oggie, and he grabs the book and shoves the picture into my face, roaring like a dragon. "ROOOOOOARRR!"

Despite my best efforts, I bust up laughing.

"Hey! Quit it, you two! You're worse than Zeek and Axel! We can't afford to get this wrong!" Mindy fumes.

Oggie holds up his hands to surrender. "Okay, okay. I'm just tryin' to have a little fun, Mindy."

"Everyone's always just trying to have fun!" huffs Mindy. "I've worked too hard to let a couple of goof-offs get me kicked out of the academy! Now can I continue, please?"

"Go ahead, Mindy." Daz shoots a disapproving glance at us.

Mindy continues reading with a sigh. "The gwarglebeast is among the most ferocious predators in the Fungal Jungle. Rarely observed in the wild, because getting too close would mean certain doom, adult gwarglebeasts can reach sizes of up to thirty feet tall and fifty feet long including its tail."

We all look at each other with wide eyes. "You don't think they'd put a gwarglebeast in the Final Gauntlet, do you?" I say in disbelief. "That thing's massive."

"Anything's possible," Mindy replies. "Dungeoneer's Code number four: expect the unexpected."

"You can never be too prepared!" Mindy snatches the inflatable raft and stuffs it back into her pack. "Besides, you won't be cracking wise when all this gear comes in handy."

"Hey, listen to this," Daz says. "The gwarglebeast's appetite is nearly insatiable. It can consume one ton of food per day, primarily subsisting on mushrooms, mandrakens, spongosaurs, and mushrums."

"Wait, what's the difference between mushrooms and *mushrums*?" inquires Oggie.

Mindy thumbs through the pages like a maniac, and I wave away all the dust she's kicking up. "I think mushrums are the local inhabitants of the Fungal Jungle," she says. "Check it out."

Fig. 110. Mushrum Folk

"The mushrums are extremely cautious and reclusive," Mindy reads, "and no one has ever observed them in their mushroom city, which is thought to be hidden deep in the Mushroom Maze."

"With a gwarglebeast on the prowl, who *wouldn't* be reclusive?" I joke.

"Well, I think we got what we need," says Mindy as she snaps the giant book shut.

"Wait. Before we go," I say sheepishly, "can we look something else up?"

"I thought you were the one who wanted to get out of here as fast as possible," mocks Oggie.

"What do you want to research?" Mindy asks.

I look at everyone and take a deep breath. "Dorian Ryder."

"Really, Coop? Again with Dorian Ryder!" Oggie shakes his head. "Just forget him already."

"I—I just want to know what happened. He was the only other human at Dungeoneer Academy. I don't want to turn out like he did."

"Would that really be something we could research in the library?" Daz wonders.

"Wait!" Mindy exclaims. "It was a big news story! I bet we could look it up in *Dungeoneer Magazine*. They keep every issue archived in the periodicals section."

Mindy leads us to a massive wall of file cabinets filled with old magazines, gazettes, and newspapers. She finds the D section for *Dungeoneer Magazine*. "Here they are! Every issue ever published."

We start opening drawer after drawer, running our fingers across the labels marking the magazines by date.

"When was Dorian expelled?" I ask.

Mindy scrunches her nose. "About five years ago, I think. Long before any of us were here."

"Wait! Here it is!" Oggie tugs issue 244 out of the drawer. "Let's check out these old Shane Shandar comics first!"

"Oggie!" Daz scolds.

"Give me that!" Mindy snatches the magazine away and flips through the pages until she finds an ominous headline.

CATASTROPHE
AT DUNGEONEER ACADEMY!

Dorian Ryder

Famed adventure school Dungeoneer Academy faced disaster during their annual Final Gauntlet test when four students were seriously injured by explosions on the obstacle course. Dorian Ryder, a competing student at the school, was responsible for sabotaging trap devices and was immediately expelled for causing the incident.

Headmaster Geddy Vel Munchowzen stated, "This particular student failed to uphold the code of conduct we cherish at our academy, and we are shocked, appalled, and disappointed." The four injured students were in critical condition but are expected to make a full recovery.

"Explosions . . . ," I mutter.

Oggie puts a hand on my shoulder. "Whoa, that's pretty serious stuff."

"Those kids could have died." Daz is stunned.

"Come on, we should get out of here." I feel a little unnerved, like suddenly there are eyes watching from the dark corners of the library.

"Wait. There's more. . . ." Mindy continues reading the article. "This is not the first time Dungeoneer Academy has faced catastrophe in recent years. Previously, Headmaster

Munchowzen's own former protégé and cofounder of the school, Lazlar Rake, was banished after three students were killed while under his negligent leadership during an unauthorized exploration mission into the Shimmering Shar. When asked again about the incident, Munchowzen declined to comment."

"Lazlar Rake?" I wonder aloud.

"Shhh, what was that?" Daz's ears perk up, and there's a **THUMP** from somewhere in the library, followed by pitter-pattering footsteps.

"Someone's coming," whispers Mindy.

"I knew this was a bad idea," I hiss.

"Go, go, go," shouts Daz.

We shut the magazine and dash through the rows of shelves, but Oggie trips and collides into one of them, knocking over a tall stack of books. He tries to pick them up and put them back in place, but I grab his arm and tug. "Forget the books! We'll be spider food!"

"Would you stop it with the spider food," Oggie exclaims. "Mr. Fang isn't gonna—"

And that's when something gooey drips on my hand from the darkness above. I whip around and look up.

There he is. Mr. Fang in all his menacing glory. He's crawling down toward us from a tall, tall bookshelf, his mandibles dripping with spit. All the blood drains from my face, like Mr. Fang's, well . . . *fangs* have already sucked the life out of me.

His long, hairy front legs look like they're reaching for me! I shut my eyes and brace for death!

The next few moments are a blur. My legs go numb, but somehow they carry me through the exit, out of the library, and back to the dorms.

"Well, that was exciting!" Mindy says, panting. "I'd call that a success!"

"Yeah, not a bad night," Daz says with a yawn. "Anyway. I'm going to get some shut-eye. Tomorrow's a big day. See ya in the morning." She stretches her arms and yawns again, then makes her way into the girls' dormitory with Mindy.

"How you doin', Coop?" laughs Oggie. "Oh man, you shoulda seen your face!"

My face is still twisted with fright. I'm almost lost for words.

"Daz is right, though. Should get some sleep. You coming, buddy?" Oggie says.

CHAPTER

10

W E'RE LATE!"
I jolt awake, scramble over the covers, and leap
off the top bunk. "Oggie! Get up! We slept in!"
With a swift tug I tear off Oggie's quilt. "I said wake up!"

"Quit it, Coop! It's too early." Oggie groans and slowly
curls into an enormous furry ball on his bed.

"It's not early! We're gonna miss our ride! The sputter-
train is leaving in less than ten minutes!"

Oggie's eyes snap open, and he tries to stand up but
knocks himself in the head. "Yow!" he growls. "How'd we
sleep in?"

For starters, I'm not sure I slept at all in the first place,
thanks to a combination of excitement for the Final Gauntlet

and horrible nightmares of being webbed by Mr. Fang! Not what I'd call a good night's sleep.

In seconds I'm dressed, and my pack is stuffed with gear. I toss Oggie's dragon shield to him from across the room. "Let's go, slowpoke! We're going to miss the Final Gauntlet!"

My head is spinning. The rest of the class must already be at the sputter-station! We bolt down the hallways of the academy, passing through Cadet Hall, where a group of older kids laugh and holler at us. "Don't be late, recruits!"

Cutting through the cafeteria, we zoom past some scouts in line for Blorf's breakfast spread. Of course, Oggie can't help but grab a boiled cackletrice egg and scarf it down.

"Don't be late, don't be late!" I gasp, echoing the snarky cadet, running so fast, I can hardly breathe.

Luckily, we arrive just in time. The sputter-train, which is this amazing clockwork locomotive that runs on rails, is already being loaded with all our classmates and teachers. Plumes

of steam spout from the smokestacks, and teams of shrym engineers rush to prep the vehicle for departure.

Only trouble is, the last seats left are next to Zeek and Axel. Apparently, not even the other members of the Red Team want to sit next to those two.

"Would have been a shame if they'd missed the Gauntlet, eh, Axel?"

"Yeah, a real shame," Axel agrees with a hiss.

"But, you know . . ." Zeek puts a long green finger on his chin and continues sarcastically, "Maybe it would have been better if they'd saved themselves the trouble. Then they wouldn't have to *embarrass* themselves in front of everybody when they fail and get kicked out of the academy."

"Haw, haw! Nice one, Zeek!" Axel replies with a nasally grunt.

To my surprise, Daz and Mindy arrive behind us. Mindy's backpack is so stuffed, it looks like it ate another backpack. Seriously, it's, like, twice her size and overflowing with adventure gear.

"Daz! Mindy! You're here later than we are! How's that possible?"

Mindy pants and drops her backpack. "Had to make sure we had all the essentials. Double- and triple-checked!"

MINdy's ESSENTials

LAVA PROOF

Zeek rolls his eyes. "Looks like a bunch of junk to me! Lava-proof raft. Really?"

"Shut up, Zeek," Oggie barks, lifting Mindy's backpack with ease.

Zeek just grins and pats the seat next to him. "Come on, Green Team. Have a seat. This could be the last time we sit next to each other. I wanna *relish* it."

I grudgingly plop down next to Zeek as he and Axel snicker with glee. I have to be on guard. Who knows what shenanigans they might pull?

The sputter-train's engines roar, and we lurch forward. Slowly at first, we roll on the tracks, bouncing over the rails,

ALL ABOARD! Next stop, FUNGAL JUNGLE!

out of the Dungeoneer Academy campus. The sputter-train whirs and clicks with clockwork gears, shuddering as it gains speed and approaches a pair of giant double doors.

"This is incredible!" I whisper to myself.

The engines pick up speed, the steam whistle blaring over all the mechanical pings and tings.

"Never been on the sputter-train before?" Daz asks.

"Nope," I say, eyes wide.

"Psh! Loser," Zeek says with a toothy grin.

"Haw! Good one, Zeek." Axel chortles.

"Better hold on, then," Daz replies with a smile, ignoring Zeek and Axel completely.

A strange, automated voice crackles through speakers in the sputter-car. "W-w-welcome aboard, students! Fasten your safety belts, secure your belongings, and clench your butts as we prepare for our descent. And don't forget to p-p-please keep your hands, feet, claws, and noses inside the sputter-train at all times! Initiating entrance procedure!"

"Opening doors!" The enormous double doors rumble open, revealing a dark tunnel. "Engage d-d-descent!"

The rush of the wind tousles my hair as the sputter-train spirals deeper below the surface. I've never seen anything like this. *Here we go,* I think. *This is it.*

Have you ever been so excited that your brain feels like it's unraveling into a big noodle, and your heart starts using your unraveled noodle brain to jump rope? Or your stomach gets so lightweight and fluttery that you feel like, if you could just run fast enough, you'd take off like a bird?

Maybe it's just me . . . but I AM that excited. Because today is my big chance. Today I take my first step toward becoming Coop Cooperson, dungeoneer extraordinaire!

I can't help but be amazed at how far I've come. Coop Cooperson, the eldest kid of sixteen. A *wonderful onesie,* as my mom would say, amidst an army of twins and triplets (except for Donovan, of course, but he's just a baby). I always kind of felt like the odd one out. Not to mention it's easy to get lost in the mix. The truth is, everyone else in the family was pretty content, but I knew deep down that I wanted something else for myself. Don't get me wrong. I love my family. I just don't want to be cooped up in a barrel all the time. (And just so you know, that pun was totally intended.) But seriously, I always saw something different for myself. I always craved adventure.

Professor Clementine's voice crackles over a speaker in the sputter-car. "For those of you who have never visited the Underlands beyond our humble academy, spare a moment to take everything in."

Oggie elbows me. "Check that out, Coop!"

"What is that thing?" I blurt out.

"No idea, buddy," Oggie replies, eyes wide with wonderment. "No idea at all."

Professor Clementine clears her throat. "The Underlands are far bigger than a few interconnected cave networks. Really, the Underlands are a world all their own. A world beneath the one we know, where thousands of creatures, critters, and species intersect. The Underlands are an amazing ecosystem, and an adventurous frontier just begging to be explored and protected. And our duty as future dungeoneers is to do just that. . . ."

The sputter-train splashes under a massive rocky, subterranean waterfall. Cool blue light washes over everyone in the sputter-car as more of those insect creatures skitter on the drippy rocks.

"They remind me of crawlbads," I say to myself.

"What's a crawlbad?" Oggie asks, overhearing me.

"Oh, it's like this huge crayfish creature that lives back home, in the River Country," I say. "It's got big claws and eight legs and wild, dangly antennae."

The crawlbad

Suddenly I'm transported back to my childhood. To all those hot summers on the bayou with my brothers and sisters. A wave of memories floods my mind.

"I remember this one time we all went crawlbad fishing back home and my little brother Chip got lost in the river reeds. We looked everywhere but couldn't find him.

"It was getting dark. I knew he would be scared, so I ran off on my own to search for him, dredging through the mud, wading through the water. I ended up getting lost myself. . . ."

"What happened?" Oggie asks.

"Well, after hours of searching, I heard him crying in the distance. I called out to him, 'Chip! Chip!' And when I found him, he was trapped in a crawlbad nest, surrounded by the biggest crawlbads you've ever seen. Their pinchers were razor-sharp, their shells blazing red in the twilight."

I realize everyone on the sputter-car is listening to my story now. Even Zeek and Axel.

"Well, what'd you do?" Daz asks intently. "What happened next?"

"I held up my stick and I charged them. Me against half a dozen crawlbads. I must have startled them, because the crawlbads just skittered away and splashed into the water. I don't know exactly what came over me, but I know in that moment, all that mattered was my little brother. He was so scared. I had to do something."

"Yeah, right!" Zeek mocks. "Coop Cooperson? Captain Hesitation? That never happened. You probably went crying to your mommy."

"It *is* true," I say. "I swear. I even found a gold coin in the crawlbads' nest."

"Oh, wow," Zeek jeers. "One whole gold coin? That's practically a dragon's hoard! Psh!"

"Well, it was a lot of money for the Cooperson family back home in River Country. So I grabbed it and got Chip outta there, and my family was ecstatic. Kept calling me Coop the Adventurer."

"Whatever. More like Coop the, uh . . ." Zeek stumbles on his insult. "The Adventure . . . *nerd*. Heh, yeah."

Everyone's quiet. Even Axel shrugs in Zeek's direction.

In that moment I realize just how much I miss my family. But I can't dwell on that now. We pass through another waterfall, and on the other side, giant multicolored mushrooms sprout from the rocks. The Fungal Jungle. Looks like we're almost there.

"You ready?" Oggie asks.

I shift in my seat, gazing at the multitude of mushrooms.

Yep. I'm Coop Cooperson. I was born ready.

11

THE SPUTTER-TRAIN ZOOMS OUT OF A rocky tunnel, click-clacking away on the tracks. Below us a huge expanse of giant mushrooms stretches as far as the eye can see. And high above the jungle canopy, rays of light from the surface world beam down through unseen cracks in the earth.

I'm jotting down all the notes of our trip so far in my journal when Professor Clementine's voice buzzes and pops over the loudspeaker again.

"Welcome to the Fungal Jungle, class," she says. "A vast domain of sprawling mushrooms, some of them taller than the tallest goblin skyscrapers."

My mind reels at the thought of new, undiscovered creatures. Imagine the possibilities! The adventure! This is exactly why I wanted to become a dungeoneer!

"But it wasn't always this way," Professor Clementine continues. "Long, long ago, the Fungal Jungle was ruled by the mushrums, a species of fungal folk that dwell deep in the hidden recesses of the biome. It is said that the Great Mushrum King once wielded the mighty Crystal Blaze, a legendary sword of immense power used only by the worthiest of heroes throughout Eem's history."

"Hey, she's talking about Mike-the-mega-whatsa-mahoozit," says Oggie, nudging me.

"And with the Crystal Blaze," Professor Clementine says, "the Mushrum King quelled the ferocious beasts that dwelled here, and tamed the jungle. For centuries, the mushrums lived in peace. But a great unknown calamity took place, and the sword was lost. The Fungal Jungle became wild once again, the way it is today, and the mushrum people retreated to their hidden homes deep within the Mushroom Maze. Or so the legend goes. . . ."

My hand can barely keep up with all the information as I scribble in my journal. I look out of the corner of my eye to see Zeek peering down at what I'm doing.

"What are you writing, Pooperson?"

I reach for my journal, but Zeek shoves his wiry hand into my face.

"Give it back!" I say.

"No way, Pooperson! Hey, Axel, listen to this." Zeek starts reading in a silly voice that's supposed to sound like mine: "'A shudder goes down my spine as the monstrously huge Mr. Fang glares at me. I see my horrified reflection quadrupled in his black eyes. I gulp. Spiders *really* creep me out.'"

The two of them burst out laughing. "What a weenie!" jeers Axel.

"You really are hopeless, Cooperson." Zeek grins.

"Would you two quit it?" Oggie says. "Just give it back."

"And look at these lame drawings," says Axel. "You drew these, harebrain?"

Oggie gets up, but Axel kicks him, and Oggie stumbles back into his seat.

"Wait, wait! Get a load of this!" Zeek chortles as he flips through the book. "OH MAN . . ."

And then it happens. Worst nightmare number three.

A sharp and tingly pang cuts through my gut like a knife, and my face feels like it's on fire. My eyes lock with Daz's.

"What a loser! I *like* like her!" Zeek mocks triumphantly. "Cringe!"

"I got news for you, dude!" Axel laughs. "Daz is way outta your league."

I finally manage to wrestle my journal away as the two bullies just laugh.

I can feel my eyes start to water. But I'm NOT giving Zeek the satisfaction of seeing me cry, so I just stare down at the floor. I don't even want to see Daz's face right now. She's probably more mortified than I am!

Then, out of nowhere, there's a big **BOOM** and a **CRACK!**

The sputter-train shudders violently. Everyone in our car gasps as we bob from side to side. I don't know what's going on. There's a horrible sound of tearing metal, almost like the screech of some terrible beast. And for a split second I look out the window, and I almost think I do see a beast. Something shadowy and huge barreling through the jungle beneath us.

And that's when things go topsy-turvy.

All of a sudden our sputter-car careens off the rails, and time seems to grind to a halt. I see the rest of the sputter-train, with Professor Clementine and the others, tumble off the rails too, but our cars have separated. Splintered wood rains down on us from where the railway has shattered and crumbled.

You know that old cliché of having your life flash before your eyes? Well, it's kinda true. I see my family perfectly in my mind. I see Mom and Dad in the kitchen cooking up a crawlbad feast. I see Chip and Flip and Kip as we all race up a tree on a cool autumn day.

Then in an instant my whole world shrinks back to the sputter-car as it plummets toward the ground. It's hard to see anything but the frightened faces of my best friends as we spin. Oggie grabs my hand, and we clutch our seat belts for dear life.

Before I lose consciousness, my eyes meet Daz's again, and I think for a moment that maybe it's not such a bad thing that she knows I *like* like her.

CHAPTER

12

MY HEAD IS FUZZY. DUST SWIRLS AROUND, obscuring my vision. I hear noise, but it all sounds muffled like I'm underwater. "Where am I?" I groan, struggling to pick myself up off the ground.

My foot's caught between two splintered pieces of wood. I manage to wrestle it free without twisting my ankle. "Is everyone okay?"

"Yeah, I think we're all okay," Oggie says, rubbing his head.

"What happened back there?" Daz asks, dusting herself off. "Did the whole sputter-train go off the rails, or . . . ?"

"Sputter-trains don't just go off the rails," I say. "Were we attacked or something?"

Daz furrows her brow. "You mean like sabotage?"

"I don't think so. It looked like something destroyed the railway—like a creature," says Mindy, who out of all of us seems completely fine. That huge backpack of hers seems to have broken her fall.

"Yeah, I saw it too. Something BIG," Oggie adds, shaking the dust off his fur. "Crashed right through the rails, and just like that! POW! No more railway."

I scratch my head. Maybe I did see a beast. Is that even possible? "That would have to be a REALLY big something."

"It could have been those toadstool trees that toppled over." Mindy gestures to our surroundings. Huge mushrooms loom over us, their enormous spongy caps blocking out the glittering cavern ceiling hundreds of feet above us. Colorful, flat spores of blue and green float in the air like weirdly shaped snowflakes, drifting between twisty, fuchsia mushrooms and massive orbs of fungus with giant holes punched through them.

"I think something *made* the toadstool trees topple," Daz replies. "Now that I think of it, I definitely saw something moving."

Mindy eyes the cluttered fungal horizon. "Well, whatever it was, we should find the others. Professor Clementine will know what to do."

"Where are they?" I ask.

"Yeah, where is everyone else? I hope no one's hurt—" Daz is suddenly interrupted by a tremendous **CLANG** followed by a screaming voice.

"Help! Get me out of here!"

"It's Zeek!" I dive through a cloud of dust to find Axel straining to lift a snarled metal beam off Zeek.

"Over here!" cries Axel. "We need help!"

Without hesitation we jump in to help and position ourselves under the beam. "Ready?" I shout. "Lift on three. One. Two. THREE!" With all our might, Axel, Oggie, Mindy, Daz, and I lift up the beam. The metal groans as we manage to raise it only a few inches off the ground.

"Can you . . . can you slide free?" I grit my teeth. The weight is tremendous. This would probably be impossible without Oggie or Axel.

"I think so!" Zeek wriggles out from under the wreckage with a yelp. "I'm out!" He falls backward, arms outstretched and panting. We let the beam go with a crash.

"Zeek, are you hurt?" I ask, patting him down.

"Get off me, Pooperson!" he cries out, shoving me away. Then he stands up abruptly, a startled look on his face.

"Help! HELP!" Zeek yells at the top of his lungs, flailing his arms and pacing back and forth. "Can anyone hear us? Professor Clementine! Mr. Fang!"

"Quit it, Zeek!" Oggie snaps. "Daz is right. We don't know what smashed the railway! We shouldn't draw attention to ourselves."

"We need to calm down and be smart," I say. "We don't know what's out there. Heck, for all we know there could be some giant monster about to—"

ROOOOOARRRRRR!

The word "attack" is utterly drowned out by the loudest roar I've ever heard in my life. It just keeps piling on, doesn't it?

133

First the sputter-train crashes somewhere in the Fungal Jungle and our whole class goes missing. And now there's a giant monster on the prowl. Probably hungry for a human, I bet.

"Um. That's not good." Oggie gulps.

"Quick, grab your stuff and run!" I yell.

We all pick up what we can from the wreckage and sprint through the jungle, away from the bellowing sounds of the monster. We dash through corkscrew stalks of fungus and leap over knots of speckled, spongy mushroom caps. After what seems like forever, we take cover in this weird jungle-gym-looking mushroom. The toadstool trees drum together like giant river reeds, and the ground rumbles as the beast draws nearer.

BOOM, BOOM, BOOM!

We're all quiet. But I can feel the tension rise as whatever is lurking in the Fungal Jungle seems to stop moving. I'm not certain of it, but I think I hear the low huffing and puffing sound of a big animal breathing. It must be hunting us!

Somewhere above, we hear skittery clicking sounds. Everyone is holding their breath, ready for the worst, when one of those crablike insects I saw before, red and shiny, crawls down from above us. We stare at it. It stares back with black, unwinking eyes, swiveling its head. Suddenly it leaps onto Zeek's leg!

Zeek's eyes lock onto the bug, and he goes rigid. The color drains from his face, and his eyes roll back. For a second I think he'll pass out, but then he starts to scream.

I cover Zeek's mouth with my hand. "Shhh!" I hush him frantically.

But Zeek wrestles free and screams at the top of his lungs. The insect creature leaps up again, but this time Zeek smacks it and the bug goes flying until it hits the ground.

POK!

"Well, that was close." Zeek laughs nervously as we all scowl at him.

Suddenly there's a thunderous **THUMP** as a toadstool tree topples over, and hundreds of those hidden red insects skitter in random directions along the jungle floor.

Then, from the swirling dusty destruction, the BIG SOMETHING finally shows itself.

ROOOOOOOAAAAAAAAR!

The beast we all feared stomps into view and roars, before snatching up a mouthful of bugs and swallowing them whole!

"I can't believe it. . . ." Daz leans forward, her words little more than a breathy whisper. "That's a gwarglebeast. . . ."

The monstrous creature opens its powerful jaws wide enough to scoop up two more crab-bugs and then bellows with what I can only imagine is delight as it swallows them down. The beast spins in place, and its gigantic tail knocks down

STOMP

STOMP

another toadstool tree before its powerful haunches propel it forward. Leaving behind terrible clawed footprints, the gwarglebeast vanishes into the dense jungle.

We're all stone-cold quiet when Zeek jumps up, hands raised. "Well, I'm out of here!"

"He's right," I say to the others. "We should collect the gear and head in the direction of the railway. That'll be our best chance to find the rest of the class."

"Which way is that?" asks Oggie.

"I . . . I'm not sure," I admit.

"We've gotten all turned around," Mindy says, adjusting her enormous backpack.

"Well, we should be able to find it if we work together," I say.

"No way," Zeek says. "Red Team only."

"Wait, what?"

"Red Team only. No way we're teaming up with you losers down here. You'll just slow me and Axel down." Zeek scoffs, "You washouts are on your own."

"What are you talking about?" I cry. "This isn't the Final Gauntlet, Zeek. We need to work together. Dungeoneer's Code five: never split the party!"

"Coop's right." Mindy pushes up her glasses and steps beside me. "We need to coordinate our skills."

"We should really stick together," Oggie says, holding his dragon shield.

"Oh yeah?" Zeek snarls. He swipes the canteen from my hand and dumps the water out in front of me. "The way I see it, this is war. Red Team versus Green Team. You're all just deadweight."

Maybe we should stick around.

Shut up, Axel! We're going.

As Zeek steps away, I place my hand on his shoulder. "Zeek. We're on the same team."

"Don't touch me!" Zeek rips my hand away and pushes me to the ground.

Suddenly I'm so angry, I'm seeing red stars.

"Coop, don't!" Oggie cries out, but I'm already off the ground and lunging toward Zeek.

"What—you wanna fight now?" Zeek smirks.

Do I want to fight? Zeek is skinny, but he's still bigger than me. And I've never actually been in a fistfight before, not outside of sparring in Combat and Tactics class, anyway. But I have to stand up for myself, don't I? I can't let Zeek keep bullying me forever. Why can't he just be reasonable for once?

"Go ahead, Pooperson. Take your best shot." Zeek fake yawns and juts out his chin. "Go on, take a swing at me. Or are you just going to stand there like a dweeb?"

"W-why do you have to be such a bully all the time?" I stammer. My hands are clenched, but I just can't bring myself to raise them.

"'W-w-why do you have to be such a bully?'" Zeek repeats mockingly, and grabs my shirt. "Maybe because a no-good, river-rat human like you should never have gotten into Dungeoneer Academy. You don't belong here. You're destined to be a washout like Dorian Ryder. You just don't know it yet!"

"Leave him alone, Zeek!" Daz steps forward. "How many times do we have to do this before you learn your lesson?"

"Back off, Daz," I say. "I've got this." The words come out, and I know they don't sound like me, but I'm embarrassed. I'm angry. Daz frowns.

"You should listen to your girlfriend, Pooperson." Zeek grins with those sharp teeth.

"You don't s-scare me, Zeek," I stammer again, but this time I'm fighting back tears.

"Yeah, you're not scared?" I watch Zeek draw back his

fist, and before I can dodge, it connects squarely with my nose. **CRUNCH.** I feel a rush of blood spurt out, and I fall to my knees.

HA
HA

Then why are you CRYING?

And I *am* crying. Tears roll down my cheeks, and blood runs down from my nose.

Zeek snorts and spits on the ground before hoisting up his pack and hiking off. "Come on, Axel. Hurry it up. Pooperson and the Green Team can rot for all I care."

Axel glances back at us and shrugs. "See ya" is all the dratch says before disappearing with Zeek into the Fungal Jungle.

"You okay, Coop?" Oggie is floored. He helps me up as I wipe the blood from my nose. "That guy isn't just a jerk. He's like . . . the king of all jerks."

Daz hands me a handkerchief. "Here, Coop."

"Thanks."

"Psh! He hopes we rot!" Oggie scowls. "Well, I hope they fall into a pit and get eaten by the gwarglebeast."

"Oggie!" chides Mindy. "That's a terrible thing to say. Not that I don't agree with the general sentiment . . ."

"Let's just hope they stay safe," I say, collecting myself.

Daz sparks a torch. The flame whooshes to light and crackles in the damp air. "Speaking of safe, we'd better keep moving. No telling if the gwarglebeast is coming back."

CHAPTER

W E'VE BEEN WALKING IN CIRCLES FOR hours," whines Oggie. "Shouldn't we have found the railway by now? I'm startin' to get hungry."

"Yeah, we should have," I say, hopping over a spotted mushroom cap. "But we can't see a thing with all these toadstool trees blocking the view. Maybe if we turn around and head north." I spin around in place. "Or is that north over there?"

I scan our surroundings, and can't make heads nor tails of where we might be. Massive stalks of toadstools climb into the air, speckled with red and orange spots. They're like trees, but instead of leaves or branches, humongous mushroom caps crown the tops. Their strange gills gently

sway in the wind and almost look like they're breathing. I watch spores float on the air like snowflakes, spinning on fluffy tendrils that smell kind of like freshly baked bread. It makes my stomach rumble. It makes me think of home.

"Face it," Daz sighs. "We're lost. Running from that gwarglebeast sent us down the wrong path."

"We're not lost," Mindy replies, examining her compass and a makeshift map she's been scrawling. "Well, correction— we *are* lost. But I think I know exactly *where* we're lost."

"Okay, start making some sense, Mindy," Oggie complains as he plops down on a toadstool.

Mindy looks us all dead in the eyes, one by one. "I think we're lost in the Mushroom Maze," she says gravely.

Suddenly my mouth goes dry, and I'm really wishing Zeek hadn't poured out my water. "The Mushroom Maze?! Do you mean the place where dungeoneers enter, never to return? *That* Mushroom Maze?"

"Are you sure?" asks Daz, echoing my fears. "You do realize, if that's true . . . that's, like, extremely bad."

"I know," Mindy replies. "But I've been observing the various fungi as we travel, and a couple of the mushrooms I just noticed match the rare species that are said to be found only in the Mushroom Maze."

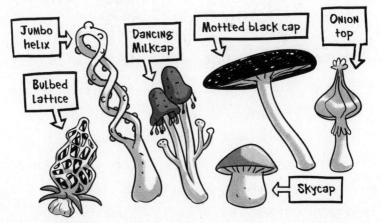

"So what does this mean?" Oggie inquires. "We're definitely going to miss lunch, aren't we?"

"Lunch?" Daz scoffs. "You're worried about lunch? Oggie, we have much bigger things to worry about than lunch."

"What? Like dinner?" Oggie whines. "You don't think we're gonna miss DINNER, do you?"

"Oggie, don't worry. I brought sandwiches, okay?" Mindy says, rummaging through her backpack. After a moment, she furrows her brow. "Wait a minute, where are they?"

Oggie bites his lip sheepishly. "Y-you mean the peanut-butter-and-mung-jelly sandwiches? I—I kinda ate those already."

"You WHAT?" Mindy blurts. "How? *When?* There were four sandwiches in there, Oggie!"

"I know. . . . I—I got nervous. And when I'm nervous, I get hungry, and I just start eating things. And before I realized it, all the sandwiches were gone."

"And you're *still* hungry?" Mindy asks incredulously.

"Well, yeah. I'm still nervous, aren't I?"

"I'm not sure you're quite grasping the seriousness of our situation," Daz sighs.

"Isn't it pretty serious that we don't have food?" replies Oggie. "You need food to live, Daz. Let's use our brains here."

"I *am* using my brain, but I don't know that I can say the same about you! If you haven't noticed, we're lost. No food, no shelter—"

"Hey . . . come on," I say, standing between Oggie and Daz.

"Let's get ahold of ourselves. We're all in this together, aren't we? Dungeoneer's Code number nine: cooler heads prevail. We've just got to remain calm and collected."

Daz is about to yell at Oggie, but catches herself and exhales deeply. "Fine," she says.

Oggie looks down and scuffs his foot in the dirt. "Sorry I ate the sandwiches, Mindy. . . ."

"Forget it," Mindy says. "It's in the past now."

"All right," I say, clapping my hands. "Our main priority is to stick together and get back to safety."

"Agreed!" Oggie straightens up, and a big rumble echoes from his belly, kind of like a tiny gwarglebeast is trapped inside. We all can't help but laugh, even Oggie.

"Let's find some food," says Mindy. "In the library I jotted down some notes about what mushrooms should be edible. We just have to keep an eye out."

"Well, let's go, fearless leader," Daz says to me, and I'm taken aback.

I look to Oggie and Mindy, who stare back at me expectantly. Me? Leader? I mean, let's totally disregard the fearless part, because we know that's not true. But they all seem to be waiting for *me* to lead the way.

"O-okay," I say. "Let's go."

We spend another hour or so trudging through the underbrush before Mindy spots an edible mushroom from her list. Something small, plump, with a powder-blue cap. I'm not much of a mushroom guy, but it's looking kinda tasty at this point.

"I think these are called skycaps," Mindy says. "Apparently, just one will keep you full for most of the day."

Oggie plucks one from the ground. "Maybe I should take a few, then. Bugbear appetite and all."

He's about to bite into it when suddenly—

"It's got a face!" Oggie exclaims, stumbling backward. "The mushroom's got a face!"

I look down at the ground and see that the whole patch of mushrooms is now crying in unison. These are babies!

"Whoa! Maybe these aren't skycaps after all," says Mindy.

"Ya think?! I almost ate, like, a person or something!" Oggie exclaims.

We start to back away, but before we can leave, an array of crystal weapons juts out from the bushes surrounding us. And holding the weapons are creatures that look like walking mushrooms. They've got spindly arms and legs, and little faces under their big toadstool heads.

"Uh-oh," Mindy mutters. "I think we've encountered mushrums! And they don't seem too friendly."

CHAPTER

14

"OUCH!" A SHARP POINT JABS INTO MY SIDE. "Watch it, okay?"

We hold up our hands in surrender as the mushrums confiscate our gear, the glimmering points of their weapons crowding our faces.

A mushrum guard pokes me again with a spiky poleaxe and prods me forward. The mushrum glowers with cloudy eyes beneath the shadowy hood of its mushroom-cap head.

They all burble commands at us in a strange language that none of us can understand. "Burga'mago! Burga'mago!" Their voices sound squeaky-squashy like shoes in the mud.

"Burga'mago! Burga'mago!" The mushrums lead us on, winding through a maze of ancient toadstool trees that

151

stretch like corkscrews into the cavernous sky. Strange violet flowers that smell like licorice bloom and unfurl dozens of spore-filled tendrils as we pass through. I have a strange feeling that eyes are watching from all around us, like the Fungal Jungle itself is alive.

"What do you remember about these mushrum folk, Mindy?" I ask under my breath.

"Not much. Just that they're very reclusive," she says with an air of excitement. "They're likely taking us to their hidden city. Pretty cool, right?"

"Did you say, 'COOL'?" Oggie interrupts with a growl.

"Well, not cool that we're prisoners," Mindy replies. "Cool that we've encountered them in the first place. This is what dungeoneering is all about! Dungeoneer's Code number one:

discover new life and lost civilizations! This is exceedingly rare! I mean, for all we know, we could be the first visitors they've had in a hundred years!"

"I've got to admit," I say as a halberd jabs my back, "that does sound pretty cool."

We're led through a stone archway wreathed in colorful patches of toadstools. In the distance, spires loom over crowded streets lined with mushroom houses that appear to sprout right out of the ground.

"Um. What's that smell?" Daz asks no one in particular.

"Smells kinda like licorice," I say.

"No, it's something stewing." Daz sniffs the air.

"I smell it," Oggie says with a huff. "Delicious, right? Like gator gumbo or sabrefish soup!"

"Well, whatever it is they want from us, I don't think it's going to be good," Daz says, pointing ahead.

"Burga'mago! Burga'mago!" Our mushrum captors shout in unison now, poking us more furiously with their weapons until we emerge into a clearing filled with more mushrum folk! It seems like they've all come out of their homes into the street to greet us. Maybe they're nicer than we think?

"Wow! That smells good!" Oggie licks his lips. "Think they'll invite us to lunch?"

Emerging from a humongous building made from the stem of a bright green, funnel-shaped mushroom, a tall, large-headed mushrum strides toward us. Covered in colorful dangling cloth and jangling with charms and jewelry, this mushrum looks like some kind of leader, or an elder.

"We have to communicate with them." I step forward, startling the mushrum guards, who rally around me, waving their pole arms.

Greetings, Your Highness!

The mushrum elder thumps their staff, and all the ornaments jingle. "You . . . are betrayers of the laws that are ruling the Mushrum Kingdom. Devouring our children is what you tried to do." The elder's voice is deep, but muddy and muted, like they're talking through a wall.

"You can speak our language!" I exclaim.

"Speaking your language is something we can do easily, yes," the elder replies. "Devouring you will now be your punishment."

"Wait, wait, wait!" I cry out, and wave my hands wildly. Anything to buy us time. "We didn't eat your children. That was just a misunderstanding! We thought they were normal mushrooms. You know, like to eat? You know, like in a salad!"

"A salad is what we are not," the elder says flatly. "But you are being soup. So says the law."

The mushrum guards grab us by the arms and march us toward a boiling cauldron. Steam blasts our faces, so hot that we have to turn away. Oggie and Daz struggle to get free, but too many mushrums keep them from escaping. Mindy, on the other hand, is practically catatonic! She's just standing there, eyes darting back and forth like her brain is in overdrive.

"Wait," I plead. "One last request."

"Last requests are not being granted," the elder replies. "Devourers from above you are! No better than the terrible beast . . . the one that is called Zarakna'rawr!"

All the mushrums gasp at the sound of the name Zarakna'rawr.

"Zarakna'rawr?" I ask, but when I do, the mushrums gasp again. "Oh! You must mean the gwarglebeast!"

"Zarakna'rawr," says the elder. "Terror of the Mushroom Maze. Devourer of mushrums. Devourer of goblins and dweorgs! Zarakna'rawr the Destroyer!" The ornamental jewels jingle as the elder raises their arms. "Now, silence."

The mushrums hush and drive us up the stepladder toward the mouth of the boiling pot.

I peer down into the swirling, steaming stew. "Come on, Green Team," I squeal. "Any bright ideas?"

"I've got nothing, Coop!" cries Oggie.

Daz squirms. "Let us go!"

The mushrums are about to push us to our scalding doom when I see something spark in Mindy's eyes.

MYKO'MORGA'MEGALOMUNGUS!

The mushrums freeze. The elder freezes.

Mindy smiles to herself and repeats the word to the elder. "Myko'morga'megalomungus. I declare a royal parley in the name of the Great Mushrum King!"

With a grunt, the mushrum elder orders the guards to let us go, and we race down the stepladder.

"Way to go, Mindy!" Oggie hugs her.

"Nice work," Daz cheers.

But before we finish celebrating, the mushrum elder raises

their hands. "A royal parley is what you are declaring. We will be hearing you now. But free, you are not."

"Now what?" Mindy whispers in my direction. And suddenly I have an idea.

"Please, hear me," I say, eyes locked with the elder's. "We meant no harm but offer a way to earn our freedom."

"Speak," demands the elder.

"We will slay the Zarakna'rawr in exchange for letting us go."

Pretty bold move, eh? Nothing like promising to slay a legendarily terrible and dangerous giant monster. But you know what? Maybe we can help the mushrums.

They are stunned into silence.

"Offering to slay Zarakna'rawr . . . is what you have proposed." The mushrum elder tilts their enormous head.

"That's right," I say with confidence, my chest puffed out.

"Uh, Coop. What are you saying?" Oggie fidgets nervously. I can tell Daz and Mindy aren't so certain of my split-second decision either.

But before I can respond, the elder's voice booms. "A brave proposition. But you should be knowing that the slaying of Zarakna'rawr is nigh impossible. Perishing is what will happen to you certainly."

At this, the other mushrums coo in their odd, tootling voices. The elder tilts their head and squints. Then collectively the rest of the mushrums tilt their heads, as if they're all in sync.

The cooing grows louder and louder until it suddenly stops. The elder considers me again and nods a final time. "We are accepting your offer."

"Oh great! They accept our offer. Perfect!" Oggie says sarcastically. "We'll just hunt down and slay a gwarglebeast. Just forget the fact that they just said death was certain! No problem. Psh! Easy-peasy." Oggie grabs my collar, his eyes blazing. "What, are you—BONKERS?"

Suddenly a stern, stoic mushrum steps forward from the crowd gathered around us. The mushrum is holding a shimmering trident and strikes it against the ground. "Foreign to our lands are you. And many dangers are lurking. A guide is what you will be needing if you are to find Zarakna'rawr in the wild."

The mushrum elder seems surprised as their charms jingle. "Our finest warrior is Tymbo'zama'gowadax," says the mushrum elder, nodding. "You are being most fortunate for this act of pity." The elder then gestures to the guards. "With our weapons of crystal you will be arming yourselves. Aid you they will."

The mushrum guards pass us their pole arms with blades of various shapes. Upon closer inspection, I see that they're made from gleaming crystal fragments chipped into razor-sharp points.

"Following Tymbo'zama'gowadax is what you shall do," the mushrum elder commands. "Guiding you through the perils of the Mushroom Maze is what Tymbo'zama'gowadax will do. Luck to you."

The mushrums hum and coo in their language, and part for us as we embark on our quest to slay the gwarglebeast, or rather, the Zarakna'rawr.

"I'm not sure that was a good idea, Coop," Daz says, examining her crystal weapon. "How can we keep our word?"

"Daz has a good point. Like their leader said, slaying a gwarglebeast is, well, almost impossible," Mindy adds.

"We don't have to slay it exactly. We could trap it. Or lead it out of the Mushroom Maze," I say, my mind racing. "We'll come up with something."

A mushrum guard hands Oggie his dragon shield back. "Oh, wait. I get it," Oggie whispers. "We're agreeing to slay the Zarakna'whatzit. . . . Then we'll ditch Tymbo and hightail it out of here. Brilliant, Coop. Now, that's dungeoneering ingenuity and know-how for ya!"

"No, Oggie," I say seriously. "They may have threatened to eat us, but that was a big misunderstanding. These mushrums live in fear. Can't you see they're scared of the beast? If we can help them, we should."

"We're scared too, Coop," Oggie says. "As soon as we get out of this city, we should make a run for it."

"We're not running, Oggie. Are we the Green Team or what?" I say. "Besides, Dungeoneer's Code number eleven: Always do what's right. Even if other options are easier."

Oggie stops to think. "Wait a second. There is no Dungeoneer's Code number eleven."

"That's true. There are only ten tenets of the Dungeoneer's Code," Mindy adds with a puzzled look on her face.

"Look, you guys. These mushrums need our help," I say. "And you're right. There is no Dungeoneer's Code number eleven. But maybe there should be."

"Plus we're lost. Maybe this Tymbo can help us find our way back?" Mindy shrugs.

Led by our new mushrum guide, we emerge on the outskirts of the mushrum city, surrounded by outcrops of rock and webs of fungus that stretch over stone cliffs glittering with minerals.

Daz turns and looks at me with a determined smile. "Coop's right. We should help."

I look to the others. Mindy has got that focused, scrunched-up thinking face, while Oggie drums his shield with his fingertips.

"I'm in," Mindy says abruptly. "Not only will we help the mushrums, but we stand to learn so much about their culture! This could be scientifically and sociologically groundbreaking!" She scribbles the location of the mushrum city onto her map.

I look at Oggie. "What do you say, pal?"

"Listen, Coop." Oggie pauses. "You know you're my best friend, right? And I would do anything for you. . . ."

"What are you saying, Oggie?" I ask, guts in a knot.

Oggie claps me on the back. "Of course I'm in! Let's do this!"

Phew! I feel my insides untie themselves.

"We are suggesting that no more time is being wasted," says Tymbo'zama'gowadax. "Follow us, Overlanders." Our warrior-guide, who apparently refers to themself as "we," points their trident over the horizon of rocks and fungal blooms and begins marching forward.

CHAPTER

T URNS OUT TYMBO HAS A LOT TO SAY. ONLY,
they never look at us when they talk, and the way
Tymbo says it is all weird and jumbled.

Mindy seems to have taken a liking to them, though. She
keeps asking Tymbo all these questions about the mushrums
and their culture. I'm trailing a bit behind, and all I can hear
are her ecstatic exclamations.

"Wow! So all mushrums share a collective intelligence?"
Mindy asks excitedly.

"This is being accurate. But only when we are engaging
in the Coo," replies Tymbo.

"The Coo! This is incredible!" Mindy exclaims. "Hold
on, let me jot this down!"

As we march through the jungle, I find myself side by side with Daz. To be honest, I've kinda been avoiding her this whole time . . . you know, since Zeek read my journal out loud. Ugh—I still can't believe that happened!

I glance over at Daz as we're walking. She's got streaks of mud on her face, and little twigs are sticking out of her hair, but none of that seems to affect her cuteness.

When she looks back at me, I quickly look away.

"What?" she says.

"Uh—nothing."

"*What?*" she insists. Her eyes lock with mine, and I can't look away anymore.

I can either chicken out or nip this whole thing in the bud. The old me would probably chicken out, but I'm feeling a new confidence lately.

"So . . . about that whole journal thing," I say. "Listen, no one was ever supposed to see—"

But Daz stops me before I can finish my thought. "Don't even mention it, Coop."

"But I—"

"Seriously." She stops walking and half smiles. "We've got bigger things to worry about, right?"

"Y-yeah," I say halfheartedly. It's true. We do. But somehow this still feels pretty big.

"Besides . . . you should check out *my* diary. There are tons of things I wouldn't want you to read either." And with that, she turns and keeps walking.

My heart skips a beat, and then I think about what she just said for a moment. Does that mean Daz writes about ME in her diary?! And wait—does that mean it's good stuff or bad stuff?

I'm lost in thought the rest of the way until Tymbo stops at a cliff, where a big, shallow chasm stretches out in front of us. A series of stone pillars rising from the mushroom-covered ground below is our only path forward. Immediately I think back to the Trial Gauntlet.

Tymbo points. "This is the way that we shall be continuing," they say in a nasally voice. "From one stone to the next, we shall all be jumping in order to safely reach the other side."

"Wait . . . why do we need to jump?" asks Oggie. "Can't we just climb down the cliff and walk? It's only about twenty feet down. And all I see is mushrooms on the ground."

"Oggie has a point," Daz says. "We wouldn't have to risk falling."

Without a word Tymbo pulls out what looks to be some sort of blue carrot from their satchel and tosses it down into the chasm below. What looked to be a field of normal mushrooms on the chasm floor suddenly comes to life and devours the carrot like a pack of hungry wolves.

"Funghouls!" says Mindy.

"Funghouls?" I yelp. "What in the world is a funghoul?"

"They're carnivorous mushroom creatures! They lie dormant until something organic comes along, and then . . . well, you saw what happened to that vegetable." Mindy checks her notes. "They can't move because they're rooted to the earth, but wandering into a bed of funghouls is certain doom. Their toxic bites put their prey to sleep, at which point every funghoul in the vicinity enters a feeding frenzy."

"Yeesh." I grimace. "Okay, so we jump from stone to stone."

"Just don't do what you did during the Trial Gauntlet, Oggie, and we'll all be fine," says Daz.

Oggie turns to Daz. "What's that supposed to mean?"

"Well, it was your fault I got knocked out of the Trial, wasn't it?"

"How was that *my* fault? Those stones were all slippery with slime! I can't control that."

"All right, all right," I say, stepping between them. "What's done is done. We're here now, and we have to work together. That's the only way we're going to achieve anything." Suddenly I feel like my parents or Professor Clementine. When did I become the voice of reason?

Mindy nods. "If we work together, this will be a piece of cake."

I see Oggie take a big gulp as he eyes the funghouls. "Yeah, piece of cake."

Tymbo cocks their head to the side, clearly confused. "There will be no eating of cake. Only life or death."

"Just follow my lead, Oggie," I say as I take a step back to get a running start. Then I leap easily across the gap.

Tymbo bounds across to where I am, and Daz follows suit. Mindy removes her backpack, opting to hold it, leaving her little wings free to fly. She flutters across to us and takes a moment to catch her breath.

"Come on, Oggie," I shout. "You can do this! I'm here!"

Oggie nods. With a big running start, he jumps like he's never jumped before. It's pretty impressive, actually, how high he gets. Only problem is, he should have used a lot of that oomph for less height and more distance. Just one of his feet touches down on the platform, and for a moment he teeters on the edge.

But I'm there to grab his meaty forearm and pull him to safety.

"There, that wasn't so hard, was it?" I say.

Oggie sighs. "Oh yeah. Another millimeter and I'd have been a light snack for those man-eating mushrooms. But it was totally no problem."

The rest of the group has already made it halfway across the chasm by the time Oggie makes it to the second platform. But then he starts getting the hang of things.

"Look at me, Coop! Pretty good, eh?"

"You're doing great, buddy!" I yell back.

Oggie's standing there triumphantly, getting ready for his next jump, when I notice that the stone pillar he's on is starting to crack!

"Oggie!" I shout. "Hurry!"

"Hey, let me take my time, Coop. Sheesh!"

"No, Oggie! The rock—it's cracking!"

"Jump!" I scream.

Oggie leaps to my platform just as his pillar knocks into the one I'm standing on. Before our pillar crashes into the next one, I see that the rest of the party is almost to the other side of the chasm, just a few more platforms to clear. But it's too late. There's a chain reaction, and all the pillars fall over like dominoes.

You're probably wondering how it could possibly get worse than this. Well, I guess we could all get eaten alive by funghouls. Yeah, I suppose that would be worse than what happens next.

Instead of us falling into a bed of funghouls, the force of the crashing pillars smashes open a giant hole in the ground! Dirt and stone and flying funghouls are all tossed into the air around us as we slide down a muddy slope.

Just another day at Dungeoneer Academy, I guess.

CHAPTER

16

S PLASH!
    We plunge into brackish water. The sudden shock
    of the cold nearly takes my breath away. I have no idea
how far we fell, but the caverns above are so dark, I can't see
a thing.

Daz emerges from a whirling patch of foam, treading water
and gasping. Then Mindy floats by, clinging to her inflatable
bag like a frightened squirrel to a tree. But where's Oggie?

"Oggie!" I cry out, and my voice echoes. The damp cave
reverberates with every word and splash.

Oggie bursts out of the water, spitting like a fountain.
"I'm okay, just a little wet!" he barks, and doggy-paddles
toward us. "That was intense!"

175

"Real nice going, Oggie," Daz grumbles. "Now what?"

"It wasn't *my* fault!" Oggie whines. "The rock just cracked on me! What was I supposed to do?" Then Oggie shifts his attention away from Daz. "Wait, where's Tymbo?"

We all shoot each other worried glances.

"Tymbo! TYMBO!" Our echoes clatter like broken glass against the dank walls of the sunken pit. "Where are you?!"

"We are presently treading the water at an interval that is comfortable. Tiring will not be happening for some time, as our vigorous appendages are being well suited for sustained activity." Tymbo's massive mushrum head bobs toward us, their eyes blank and staring unemotionally.

"Phew! A simple 'Right here' would have been enough, buddy," Oggie says with a smirk.

Looking around, I see that everyone's uneasy. I also spot dry land a few hundred feet away. "Come on," I say. "There's a stony shore over there. We can dry off and figure out where we are."

"Sounds like a plan, chief." Oggie paddles toward the shore. "Hey, Tymbo, what is this place, anyway? Am I wrong, or is this water kind of salty?"

Mindy kicks her feet, using her backpack as a floatie device. "Oggie, I'd advise against drinking the subterranean pit water. . . ."

"You, the one called Oggie, are correct." Tymbo floats closer to us. "This water is belonging to the great Underdeep, a sea that is being hidden beneath the earth. Tarrying here would be folly, for there is being much danger."

"Wow," Oggie says, eyes wide. "You mean there's a whole ocean down here?"

"Dungeoneer's Code number two: explore uncharted places," I say. "We're really doing it, aren't we?"

"I can almost feel a current," Daz says, twirling in the water.

"Amazing." Mindy wipes off her spectacles and watches the water swirl and bubble with foam.

"Paddling with vigor is essential," Tymbo says flatly. "We must be hurrying to the shore. For in the Underdeep there is dwelling the dreaded—"

SPLOSH!

Suddenly tentacles slither from the water and coil around Tymbo with ferocious speed!

"Help Tymbo!" I cry, switching directions in the water to move toward our friend.

The water whirls angrily as more dark green and blue tentacles stretch from below, splashing and snaring us like coiled snakes.

"Argh! What are these things, Mindy?" Daz strikes a floundering tendril with her poleaxe.

"Scumseers!" Mindy screams, grappling with a rubbery arm. She tugs at Tymbo as more tentacles reach from the water. "Oggie! Help me! I can't hold on!"

Oggie plunges his hands into the water and grabs hold of Tymbo's torso.

We've all got our hands around Tymbo, struggling to free them from the grip of scumseers, when suddenly countless more glowing yellow eyes peer at us from below.

"We're surrounded!" Daz raises her crystal-tipped poleaxe and roars, "Fight for our lives!" before diving after Tymbo.

But the scumseers are too nimble in the water! Their sleek, slimy bodies just glide back and forth, dodging our every attack. Their tentacles wrap around our weapons and pluck them from our hands almost effortlessly.

"Our weapons!" I yell, before diving to fetch my sinking poleaxe. My hands are almost fast enough to catch it, but what I see next chills my blood, and I forget about the crystal pole arm altogether. Below us, deep in the water, dozens and dozens of writhing scumseers lurk amidst what I can only surmise are some kind of sunken ruins. The scumseers leer at me with those glowing yellow eyes through the dark, salty murk.

I break for the surface and rocket out of the water like a river dolphin. "We have to get out of the water! Now!" I gasp.

Before anyone can respond, Oggie manages to pull Tymbo free! But in the same moment, more scumseers rise from the darkness with demonic speed. Their lantern eyes lock onto Oggie and Tymbo, casting a pale yellow light over the water.

With a terrible precision, the largest scumseer, a bulbous, tentacled fiend, strikes Tymbo with a swipe of its harpoon.

I grab Oggie's hand and pull him to safety, frantically swimming for our lives. The dark water bubbles angrily all around us. Then, as we reach the shore, the roiling waters suddenly go still.

"We made it!" I gasp.

Well . . . almost all of us. Oggie has tears welling in his eyes. "Poor Tymbo."

"I know," I say, putting my arm around him. Daz and Mindy approach, and we all sit at the edge of the water.

"Tymbo . . ." Oggie's voice wobbles. "I wasn't strong enough . . ."

"It's not your fault," I reply solemnly.

Daz and Mindy stare out at the water in silence. What is there to even say? In moments like these—hard ones—something doesn't always have to be said.

My mom told me once, back when our dog Persimmon died, *Sometimes it's okay to just sit with your sadness*. Well, that's what we all do now. We sit in silence on cold stones at the edge of the Underdeep, dripping wet, tired, and lost.

"We're doomed," Mindy mutters. She stands up and paces.

"How will we ever get back to the surface?" Daz scans the darkness surrounding us. "What if we're trapped down here?"

"We just have to remember the Code," I say.

"The Code! Enough with the Code!" Oggie yells. "Nothing in the Code tells you what to do about watching your friend die." Tears flood his eyes. "We're lost. We're trapped at the bottom of this horrible pit with things skulking under the water. . . ."

Mindy sits back down, alone on a cold stone overlooking the dark water. "He's right. It's hopeless."

"It's not hopeless," I insist. "Nothing is hopeless. Don't you see? That's what hope is! We could be alone down here, but we're not. We're together—and together, there's a chance."

SPLISH!

"What was that?" Daz perks up, still on high alert.

SPLASH!

"Wait. There it is again," I say, standing up at the shore. My hands are balled up. I'm ready for a fight this time. Let's see those scumseers try that again. . . .

"Hold up, Coop," Oggie warns, standing beside me. "Is that what I think it is?"

Mindy can barely believe what she is seeing. "This is incredible. This is remarkable. Tymbo's alive! Mushrum folk can reconstitute themselves after dismemberment? By Gandy, what a marvel! Wait until we tell Professor Clementine about this."

"Amazing!" I'm blown away. First by the fact that Tymbo's alive, and second by witnessing a person divide into two people! How awesome is that?

Tymbo interrupts our celebration. "The prudent course of action is moving from this place. The danger is being . . ." Tymbo pauses, and the two halves look at each other blankly. "Extreme."

"They're right," I say, examining our surroundings. "We

need to move out as fast as we can. How are we doing on supplies?"

"Well, we don't have weapons anymore," Daz says with a frown. "So slaying a gwarglebeast could be . . . a bit challenging."

"Don't worry," I reply. "We'll just need to improvise. That's what dungeoneers do best, right?"

"So which way do we go?" Oggie asks, shaking the water off his dragon shield.

"I think I found a tunnel leading down!" Mindy shouts. "But I don't think we want to be going down. We want to get out of here!"

"Good eyes, Tymbo! Or is it . . . Tymbos?" Mindy responds, rubbing her chin.

I stare up into the tunnel and squint. "Looks like an old mine shaft or something."

"Looks like a tight squeeze." Oggie gulps.

Daz pats him on the back. "Come on, you'll be fine."

Mindy flutters up into the narrow, rocky tunnel. Old wooden boards seem to barely keep the rocks from collapsing in on themselves. "I can definitely feel a draft of air up here. I think this will lead us back to the surface!"

One of the Tymbos—yep, I guess we're calling them the Tymbos now—climbs on top of the other and springs into the tunnel to help Mindy pull us all upward.

"It is a tight fit, isn't it?" I say as a pointy rock jabs into my side.

Daz lithely climbs up the rocks, leading the way. "Step where I step. Use the wooden boards for leverage."

One after another we follow Daz. It's a hard climb up the slope, and my hands are getting sore. But finally, as we slowly crawl forward, a pinpoint of light shines brightly up ahead, and a welcome cool draft of air hits my face.

"We're almost to the surface!" Mindy exclaims.

Just as the mouth of the tunnel gets as big as my fist in the distance, a shadowy figure emerges, silhouetted by the light.

"Finally some good luck! Another person!" Oggie shouts.

"I've been looking for you." The stranger speaks, and his voice echoes down the tunnel ominously.

"Zeek? Is that you?" I ask. I've never been so happy to see him.

Daz stretches out a hand. "Can you help us out of here? Maybe throw a rope or something."

But the figure doesn't answer.

"Hello, can you hear us? A little help!" Oggie shouts, hunched between two rocks uncomfortably.

Another long pause. Maybe this isn't Zeek. But who? My gut starts to ache, which tells me something just isn't right.

"Are—are you with Dungeoneer Academy?" I ask, my voice shaky.

The stranger laughs. "No. No, I'm not." He pulls a shiny ball from the fold of his cloak. With a flick of his thumb, we hear a mechanical click. "You weren't supposed to survive the crash, let alone get away. But a plan never goes off without a hitch, does it? "

My mouth goes dry. "Plan? What are you talking about?"

"Sabotage," Mindy gasps.

"Where are the others?" shouts Daz. "Are they hurt?"

Oggie's eyes go wide. "Um—guys. He's holding a shrym grenade!"

"You won't get away with this!" Daz grits her teeth.

"Won't I? When everything's all over, there won't be a hint of evidence."

"Who are you?" I demand. "Why are you doing this?"

"We have our reasons," the stranger hisses.

"We?" I exhale. My stomach churns. My mind reels. I just keep asking myself, over and over, *What is going on? Who is "we"?*

"Time's up, dungeoneers. Consider yourselves . . . expelled." The mechanical ball stops clicking and starts humming. The stranger backs away out of sight and tosses it into the mouth of the narrow tunnel.

17

OGGIE STRAINS TO LIFT ONE OF THE boulders blocking the exit. "They're just too heavy," he continues, out of breath. "We'll never get through."

Rocks and rubble are piled up by the ton. Everyone coughs from the gray dust and floating debris.

"We have to go back," I say, peering behind us.

"Who was that guy? Why is he doing this?" Daz asks as she dusts herself off.

"I don't know, but we need to find another way out of here if we're going to help the others," I respond.

"There was another tunnel back there, remember?" Mindy says. "But it led deeper down."

"Now that tunnel is being our only option," say the Tymbos matter-of-factly.

Mindy rummages through her pack and pulls out a lantern. "This should help," she says, and guides us back to where we started, down to the Underdeep, where the Tymbos split in two. Once there, we peer into the murky, musty tunnel that will take us to who knows where.

"Yuck," Oggie sneers. "This tunnel reeks."

"Finally, a taste of your own medicine," I say with a friendly nudge.

Daz turns up her nose. "You two are gross."

"Can't argue with that," says Oggie happily.

Our shadows stretch along the dark, dank walls as we make our way slowly from the bowels of the Underdeep. The whole place smells rotten, and the air tastes like salty socks. But we trudge on in our soaked clothes as the walls and ceilings drip wet with slime.

Hours pass. We're tired and hungry. We march through tunnel after tunnel, not always certain if we're headed the right way. Then, just as I start to feel like I can't take another step, huge shimmering gems twinkle like stars above us. Prisms of colorful crystals now line the walls, reflecting our faces like mirrors.

"Wow," Oggie utters, mouth agape.

"It's beautiful here," Daz adds.

"Incredible! Look at this one!" Oggie reaches out to touch a prismatic crystal almost as tall as he is, but the Tymbos forcefully pull him back.

"Prudence is to refrain from the disturbing of the environment," they warn. "The Crystal Caverns is a place that is having danger and doom."

"What's here?" Mindy asks. But all the Tymbos reply with is "danger and doom" again. That could be said of the entire Fungal Jungle, if you ask me!

And let me tell you, it takes A LOT of effort to avoid touching anything in the Crystal Caverns. Some of the passages are really tight squeezes, with sharp crystals poking out at us.

It's like you have to be one of those circus contortionists that used to visit my town every year.

Now just try to imagine my best bud, Oggie, squeezing by that. Ain't gonna happen. So I'm sure you can guess what happens next. . . .

The crystal shatters as it hits the ground. We all stare at it, and then at the Tymbos, and then at each other, waiting for something bad to happen.

"Maybe it's fine." Oggie shrugs.

But, of course, he spoke too soon. We hear the sound of more crystals cracking, and all of a sudden a jagged shape seems to walk right out of the cavern wall itself. And then another, and another!

"They're—they're dudes made out of crystals or something!" Oggie stammers.

"Chromadytes!" shouts Mindy. "I should have known."

"Well, maybe we can talk to them," I say. I put my hands up to show we're not armed. "Um—hi! We're just passing through. We didn't mean to—"

"Trespassers!" one of them crackles. "Vandals of the Overlands." They have no faces except for a single crack that serves as their mouth.

"No, it was an accident!" I plead as we all stumble backward. And then *CRACK!* Oggie accidentally breaks another crystal.

"Oggie!" groans Daz.

The Tymbos step in front of us as the chromadytes slowly creep forward. "There no longer is the option of negotiating with the creatures of crystal . . . only battle!"

"Battle? But we have no weapons!" I argue.

"I think the Tymbos are right," says Mindy. "Chromadytes

are highly protective of their territories. We are considered enemies now."

"Why's everyone so sensitive around here? It was an accident!" cries Oggie.

One of the chromadytes swipes at the Tymbos with its jagged crystal-covered arm, but the mushrum trackers deftly dodge in opposite directions.

"Where do we go?" I shout. "These things are blocking the way, and it's not like we can turn back the way we came! It's like a maze in here!"

"Gimme your shield, Oggie," says Daz.

"What? Why?"

"Just do it." Daz takes the dragon shield, which covers about half her body, and roars, "Follow me!" Then she barrels toward the chromadytes like a battering ram.

The force of her charge knocks the chromadytes aside, buying us enough time to dart past them down the tunnel. I glance behind me and see them giving chase. This isn't going to be easy!

In the blink of an eye, we're confronted with two branching tunnels. "Which way?" pants Daz. But before I can answer, more chromadytes appear from the tunnel to the left, their sharp, pointed hands gleaming in the lantern light.

"Right tunnel it is!" I exclaim.

For a moment I think we might be in the clear, but the air starts to get humid and hot, and an orange glow flickers ahead.

When we emerge from the tunnel, the path is blocked by a river filled with hot, bubbling, orange goop.

"Lava," says Mindy. "It's a river of lava!"

Behind us a cluster of angry chromadytes clatters through the tunnels. They'll be here any second.

"So we stand and fight, then," I say.

"Not if I can help it," says Mindy, reaching into her backpack and pulling out something square shaped. With the press of a button, her little folded-up rubber raft suddenly fills with air.

We hop onto the raft, and the current of lava sweeps us away just as the chromadytes arrive.

"I think we're safe!" Oggie shouts over the rushing lava.

But the Tymbos shake their heads. "Our troubles are not being over yet, friends." They point up ahead, but I can only see darkness. "The river ends, and we will end with it."

"What does that mean?" Oggie asks.

Ahead of us, I hear a loud continuous crashing sound, and being from the River Country, I'm pretty familiar with what that means. A waterfall. Or in this case . . . a *lavafall*.

"No, but I have something else for my flightless friends," Mindy replies, this time pulling a grappling hook out of her bag. She starts swinging it at her side and eyeing the ledge. "Take my backpack, Oggie."

We can clearly see the edge of the falls now as the river

rushes us toward certain doom. Unless Mindy can make the throw of her life, we're goners!

"Hurry, Mindy," cries Daz. "What are you waiting for?"

"Perfect timing," she mutters.

For a second everything seems to be in slow motion as Mindy lets loose the grappling hook and lifts off, propelled by her wings. It's a thing of beauty.

We all cling to the rope for dear life as our feet lose contact with the lava-proof raft, which nose-dives down the lavafall.

Now we're swinging full speed across the cavern toward a hard rock wall, and I'm thinking we're all about to splat like bugs. But Oggie comes to the rescue!

Legs like tree trunks!

From there we clamber up the rope and finally reach the ledge. (Thanks to Coach Quag, I guess, for all those rope-climbing drills!) Once we get to the top, everyone just slumps to the ground, exhausted.

"We did it!" Oggie hoots. "Way to go, Mindy! You really saved our necks! We are *AWESOME*! Green Team rules!"

I high-five my best bud, but when I turn around, no one else is sharing our enthusiasm.

"Now what do we do?" Mindy says, pointing to the dead-end

crystal wall in front of us. "There's nowhere to go from here. There's no tunnel, no door! We're stuck up here, unless we want to hop into the lava river without a lava-proof raft!"

"Why's everyone so glum?" Oggie asks. "We'll find a way out of this."

"Oggie," Daz scolds. "You do realize it was *your* clumsiness that got us into all this trouble, don't you? I mean, think about it. You're the reason we fell into the Underdeep and almost got the Tymbos killed. And *you're* the one who broke the crystals, leading us to this fiasco. We almost died, like, four times because of you! And now we don't have weapons or food!"

Basically, everyone did something awesome just to make up for all YOUR mistakes. And now we're STILL stuck at a dead end. . . .

...

"Daz . . . come on," I say. "You're being too harsh. What about just now when Oggie stopped us from slamming into the wall? That was great."

"She's not being too harsh, Coop," says Mindy. "It's true! Now we'll never make it back! Everyone's probably already found each other by now. We're gonna be the only ones in the whole class who don't compete in the Final Gauntlet."

"Really, Mindy? The Final Gauntlet?" Daz says. "We're lost! Who cares about the Final Gauntlet at a time like this? Get your priorities straight. We need to worry about survival."

That seems to strike a nerve with Mindy, who turns around to Daz and points a thumb to her own chest. "Get MY priorities straight? Wow!" she snarls sarcastically. "I have my priorities straight, which means getting good grades and doing well in school! Just because you're naturally great at everything and your rich parents got you enrolled at the academy doesn't mean we can all be so lucky. I mean, you barely even apply yourself anymore, Daz!"

"Mindy, you don't know what you're talking about, okay? I'm going through some family problems. Just drop it!"

"No! Some of us worked really hard to get where we are. When all the other kids were goofing off and having fun, some of us gave it our all! Some of us studied every single day and every single night. Some of us gave up a lot. I can't let that just be for nothing!"

"Well, I guess it *was* all for nothing," Daz replies in a huff.

"Look, everyone needs to cool it," I say, trying to ease the tension. "We've all got problems, but we can work through them, okay?"

"Cool it? Problems? Yeah, right!" Daz snaps back. "Your life is perfect."

"What are you talking about?" I ask, baffled.

Daz shakes her head. "Oh, come on. Stacks of letters from your family, care packages full of treats and cookies. You don't have to worry about anything! You have the best parents in the world," she scoffs, and folds her arms. "You don't even know. I'm totally alone here."

"*You're* alone? Did you really just *say* that?" I stand there for a second, trying to fight back my tears. "I'm the only human in the whole school. Heck, I'm the only human in the Underlands! Besides Zeek and Axel, who just want to make my life miserable, you three are the only other kids who will even speak to me or look my way. It's like I'm some kind of monster."

I throw my hands up into the air. "None of you even told me about Dorian Ryder. And you're on my team! What do you say to that?"

No one says a word; they just look away.

"*I'm* alone, Daz. Living underground, a hundred miles from home, trying to be the best that I can be and make my family proud. Sure, they send me letters. But that doesn't make up for the fact that I'm an outsider. Everything I do is judged a thousand times more than anyone else."

I tear off my green neckerchief in anger. "You don't know what it's like, Daz. None of you do!"

"S-stop fighting! I'm the screwup." Oggie sniffles as tears roll down his face. "I—I screw up all the time. I know it. You know it. My dad knows it too. That's why he sent me to Dungeoneer Academy in the first place.

"'Shape up or ship out!'" shouts Oggie in a stern voice. "He used to say that every day. Well, I got shipped out so the academy could whip me into shape. But I'm just not good enough. I might be strong, but I'm not tough. And we all know I'm the biggest klutz in the world."

Oggie turns away from us, looking into the fiery lavafall. "It was all my fault, okay? Blame *me*. I know I don't belong here. All I ever wanted was to be an artist. I just want to draw and paint. Create things, you know? But all I do is ruin everything...."

"What?" I ask, my voice cracking. "Y-you can't..."

Oggie turns around and nods solemnly. "I already talked to Headmaster Munchowzen about it. I just don't belong here."

"But, Oggie, you're part of Green Team," I say.

"Who cares? It's not like it matters anymore anyway. Thanks to me, we're lost. Face it. I'm a failure, Coop."

Everyone is still quiet. Even the Tymbos don't know what to say.

Daz steps forward. She has a kind of pained look on her face. "I'm failing too," she says.

"What?" we all gasp together.

"You're failing?" squeaks Mindy. "But . . . you're practically the best student in the whole school."

"I don't know," Daz says distantly. "I thought maybe if I flunked a class or two, it might . . . it might get my parents' attention." She grimaces and fiddles with her neckerchief. "But even that hasn't changed anything. They don't care. They're always so busy, too wrapped up in their work to give me a second thought. I haven't heard from them in months.

"Look," she continues softly. "I . . . I'm sorry, Oggie. I didn't know . . . about you and your dad. I know how difficult that can be. And, Mindy, you were right, I haven't been applying myself lately. But if Oggie's a screwup, then so am I."

Mindy flutters between us. "I—I know I'm hard on you guys. Sometimes I think I can be hard on people . . . because of the pressure I feel on myself. But I'm a screwup too. I'm not strong like Oggie, I'm not graceful like Daz, and I don't have Coop's leadership ability. That means I have to be smart and prepared, and sometimes that gets really overwhelming."

"Did you say 'leadership'?" I ask, genuinely surprised. "Mindy, sometimes I get so overwhelmed by the moment that

I freeze up and don't know what to do. If anyone's a screwup, it's me."

"We are also being screwups," the Tymbos say in unison. "It was our duty to be guiding you through the Fungal Jungle, yet here we are being. Lost and certain to die of severe nutrient deficiency."

"Great, so we're all screwups," Oggie laments.

"Fantastic," sighs Daz. "Five—no, six—screwups trapped in a lava cave. Lost in the Mushroom Maze!"

I can't help but chuckle as a strange thought comes to mind. "You know, maybe being a screwup isn't such a bad thing. Maybe being a screwup is the best thing to be."

"Um, how is being a screwup a good thing?" Mindy snorts out a giggle.

"Think about it," I reply earnestly. "When you fail a lot, you learn that much faster how to do better the next time. Besides, what's better than starting from the bottom and working your way up? That's something to be proud of, right? I don't know about you, but I can't wait to show everyone else what Green Team is made of! Screwups? I'll wear that badge with honor."

I stand up and stick my hand out in the middle of an invisible huddle, waiting for my friends to join me. "Green Team on three!" I shout.

Mindy and Daz come over and place their hands on top of mine. Then the Tymbos join in.

"You with us, Oggie?" Mindy asks with a smile.

"We need you." Daz grins.

Oggie hesitates a moment. I can tell he's got a lot of things churning in his mind, and part of me is worried that maybe he really does want to leave Green Team for good. Then a wry smirk sweeps across his furry face, and he bounds over to us.

"Well," Mindy sighs. "Now that we've acknowledged that we're all screwups of some kind, maybe we should put our heads together and focus on getting out of here."

I notice for the first time the intense heat emanating from the glowing red lavafall. Sweat beads at my brow. "You can say that again! It's hot in here."

Mindy paces the area, staring at the walls and floor. "Huh. . . . I'm really not having any good ideas."

Daz peers out into the chasm. "Yeah, all that excitement, and nowhere to go."

Oggie wanders over to a stone wall and plops down on a smooth blue crystal. "Not to mention, I could really use some brain food right about now."

Then Oggie leans back against the wall, and there's a grinding sound, then a **CLACK!**

Suddenly a hidden door in the crystal wall slowly grinds open in front of us.

"Whoa!" I gasp.

"Oggie," Daz says, "did I ever tell you you're a genius?"

18

DUNGEONEER'S CODE NUMBER EIGHT: EVERY dungeon has a secret door," Mindy says with awe as the secret passageway is revealed.

We enter through the secret door and walk into a passage where veins of silver and gold shimmer. Glowing sea-green crystals grow from the walls like angular weeds. Up ahead, glittering with violet and blue speckles, there's another stone door with strange patterns carved into it.

"What do you think that pattern means?" Oggie asks, mesmerized by the peculiar glyphs. "It looks like writing . . . but incomplete somehow."

"I don't know," I answer. "It's a door for sure, but I don't see a handle." I probe the wall, my hands feeling over the contours in the stone, looking for any clue of a hidden handle or knob.

"A chromadyte door is what we are encountering," the Tymbos explain. "This is an ancient place."

"Oh no!" Mindy exclaims. "What did I do?"

"Dungeoneer's Code number six!" I answer.

Mindy finishes my thought. "Always check for traps."

"A little help over here," Daz shouts, gripping the crystal portcullis gate and striving to lift it.

We tackle the crystal gate as a team, but even with all our combined might, we can't lift it an inch. And, of course, to make matters worse? The walls start closing in on us! Classic! What's a dungeon crawl without a terrifying booby trap that will not only skewer you but also squish you into jelly?

"One more time," I grunt. We lift together, again with all our strength. But the gate doesn't budge.

"It's impossible!" Daz is panting. "We couldn't lift this if our lives depended on it."

"Well, they DO depend on it, so . . ." Oggie growls and pulls again, with even more energy and force. But no use!

"Bracing the walls is what we must do!" The Tymbos each take a side, positioning themselves between the crystal spikes. "We are requiring aid," the Tymbos grunt in unison, their spongy arms swelling with effort.

"Everyone, take a side!" I yell. "Daz with me, Oggie with Mindy!" We brace ourselves against the walls as they grind closer and closer.

"Hurry up, Oggie! I can't hold it on my own!" Mindy struggles. The wall pushes her backward, sliding her whole body across the floor.

But Oggie is just standing there, staring at the glyphs on the door.

"This is important," he mutters to himself, tongue stuck out of his mouth the way he does when he draws.

"There's no time for that! Help!" I bellow, sweat dripping as the walls close in like a monster's jaws. "Oggie!"

My feet slip as we're pushed helplessly into the spikes by the closing walls. We're doomed!

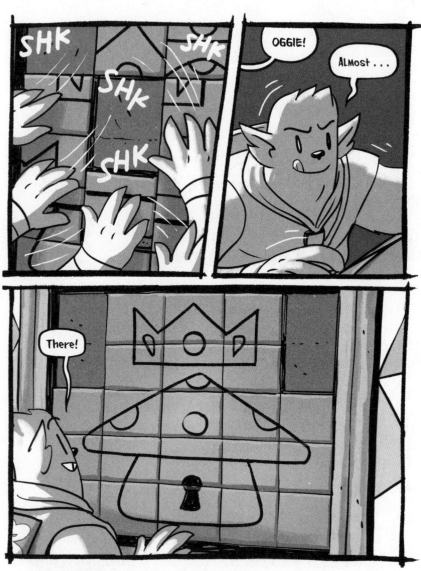

CLICK!

"Got it!" Oggie exclaims. And with a deafening **CRACK** the door activates.

The collapsing walls suddenly reverse, their spikes receding. And the crystals scattered throughout the chamber begin to blaze with violet-blue light. We collect ourselves for a moment, breathing heavily and laughing with joy.

"You did it!" I exclaim. "We're alive!"

"Incredible!" Mindy cries. "You solved the puzzle!" She flutters right up to Oggie's face and kisses him squarely on the cheek. "Daz was right, you are a genius!"

Oggie blushes. "Ah, it was nothing. Just sort of made sense, you know? Just had to complete the drawing."

Daz hugs Oggie. "Good thing we've got the best artist around."

I give his shoulder a hearty shake. "Nice work, Og!"

Oggie beams. I can tell he's got a newfound swagger, and I couldn't be happier for him.

"We are feeling a sense of amazement." The Tymbos approach the door, admiring the mushroom symbol etched into the tile-like puzzle. "What we are seeing . . . is the emblem of Myko'morga'megalomungus . . . the Mushrum King."

"Whoa" is all I can think to say. "Like in the legend . . ."

Before us lies a vast crystal chamber. Ginormous pillars of angular, translucent gemstones rise into an enormous dome. We pass through the door and emerge into what looks like the interior of a gemstone palace.

We all fan out, investigating the area, and I find myself next to Oggie.

"Hey, can I ask you something?" I feel sheepish. "Are you really gonna leave the academy?"

Oggie pauses a moment, then says, "Maybe."

"How come you didn't tell me?" My eyes are glued to the path.

218

Oggie shrugs. "What was I supposed to say?"

"I don't know. I just hope you don't."

"Hey, check this out!" Daz's voice echoes, startling us. She's bent over, examining something on the ground.

I dash over and peer down. "Looks like a pile of glittery sand," I say, unsure what I'm looking at.

"That's not sand," Mindy adds, kneeling down beside Daz.

I think this is chromadyte dust. Clearly they were inhabiting this place.

And something MUST have PULVERIZED them. But how?

"I wonder what happened." Daz pinches the crystalline powder between her fingers. "Could there have been a cave-in?"

"We are surmising that the destruction was caused by the dreaded Zarakna'rawr." The Tymbos stand side by side, pointing to massive claw marks in the stone floor. "We are certain. Yes. Zarakna'rawr."

"You mean the gwarglebeast smashed these chromadytes into dust?" Oggie gulps. "How are we supposed to stop a monster like that?"

"We'll find a way," I reply confidently. But deep down? I'm not so sure. Truth be told, shivers run down my spine when I think about the gwarglebeast. Those glaring eyes, and gaping maw, gums overstuffed with giant teeth . . . Heck, it's almost worse than a spider.

"Well, these chromadytes sure didn't fare well against it," Daz laments.

That's when I notice, as we continue forward, that the entire floor is covered with colorful, glittering grit and more huge scrapes dug out of the ground. My feet slide unevenly as I walk over the crunchy powder. "There must have been an army of them. The whole place is filled with pulverized crystals. Just watch your step, or else you'll—"

PLUNK!

I trip over something buried in the dust and fall face-first onto the floor.

"Whoa! You okay there, Coop?" Oggie picks me up off the ground.

"Yeah. But I tripped on something." I kneel down and sift through the glittering dust. I feel something sharp, and almost cut my hand.

"Weapons!" Oggie exclaims.

"Wait, do you think it's okay to take this stuff?" I ask, genuinely uncertain.

The Tymbos pick up a spear and shield, saying flatly, "We are being favored most fortuitously. We must be sufficiently arming ourselves, and reclaim what was being lost."

"Dungeoneer's Code number three: unearth and preserve our collective history," Mindy says matter-of-factly. "If we don't take them, they might be lost forever."

"And besides, what else are we gonna fight the Zarakna'rawr with?" Oggie picks up the axe and clinks it against his shield. "Whoa! Wicked dragon design! It matches my shield perfectly."

Daz twirls two dazzling daggers with gemstone pommels. "These are really well balanced."

"Ooh, sparkly!" Mindy grabs the silver gem-encrusted bow and gives it a twang. "Matching arrows too!" she continues as she puts some glittering arrows in her backpack.

"Vintage, huh?" I repeat, holding the rusty sword. Not in the best shape, I'll admit. But I suppose it'll do the trick. I wave the sword once in the air, just to make sure it's sturdy enough to wield. Satisfied, I address the party. "All right, Green Team. Are we ready?"

We traverse the hallways of the crystal palace, navigating through the vast rooms and chambers of what once was the seat of power for the ancient Mushrum Kingdom. Eventually we exit the grounds, and at last we reach a dark passage that splits into three tunnels.

"So which way should we go?" I ask, totally stumped.

Oggie and Daz both glance at me and shrug.

"I suppose we could just pick at random," Oggie suggests.

"Random?" Mindy scoffs. "No way! We're dungeoneers. Every problem has a solution, right? We just have to examine what we're dealing with here."

"But the tunnels all look the same," Oggie says.

"Oh no," I squeak. "Spiders?!"

"No, not spiders. It's mycelium!" Mindy corrects me.

"My-see-luh-what?" Oggie's face scrunches up.

"Mycelium," Mindy replies distractedly. "It's what mushrooms use to embed themselves into the ground. You know, kinda like roots."

"I get it," says Daz. "The mycelium means that mushrooms must be growing above that tunnel."

"Precisely! All we gotta do is follow the mycelium, and it should take us back to the Fungal Jungle!"

"Right on, Mindy!" Oggie gives Mindy a high five. "If I'm a genius, then you're, like . . . a super mega genius!"

Mindy blushes. "Nah, I just study a lot—"

"No longer should we be tarrying," the Tymbos say, interrupting. "Zarakna'rawr!"

"Yeah, yeah. We know," Oggie says, putting his arms around the Tymbos. "Gwarglebeast, here we come! Onward! Follow the mushroom roots!"

"That's mycelium," Mindy corrects.

Oggie makes a face and raises a finger triumphantly. "What Mindy said!"

We follow the mycelium through the tunnel toward the surface. The walls are thick with thatches of more and more webby mycelium, until at last we discover a staircase carved out of crystal. The stairs spiral upward, with mycelium weaving like thread in the ceiling. In some places it's so thick, we're forced to slice our way up the crystal stairs.

Huffing and puffing, we take a moment to breathe fresh air. Daz sits down next to me on a toadstool, while Mindy and Oggie rummage through the backpack for something.

"Hey, Coop," Daz says to me quietly. "About earlier . . . I just wanted to say . . . sorry. I was so wrapped up in my own problems, I didn't realize what you were going through."

"It's okay, Daz. I'm sorry too. I shouldn't have blown up like that." Daz smiles and brushes the bangs out of her eyes. My palms start to sweat, and my mouth feels dry. "I . . . well, I guess I just care . . . you know? I guess what I'm trying to say . . . I mean, uh . . ."

Then I notice that Daz isn't paying attention to me at all.

"Oh no! Coop, over here!" Daz shouts, and races off.

I grip my rusty sword and chase after her. "What is it?"

"Look!" Daz points to a torn red neckerchief on the ground, and my stomach drops.

"The Red Team . . . Zeek and Axel . . . ," I gasp. "They must be in trouble."

CHAPTER

WE RACE THROUGH THE JUNGLE, DAZ leading the way toward the gwarglebeast. Each time the creature howls, it sounds a bit more distant, but Daz perks up her ears and readjusts our path. She'd be great at hunting crawlbads in the River Country, that's for sure!

Soon the roar sounds close again, and Daz motions for us to stop as she silently creeps forward over the drybrush. After a moment she gives a hand signal for us to come closer. We part the massive leaves in front of us and peer through.

There it is! The fearsome gwarglebeast!

Only, it doesn't look all that fearsome right now, huddled

alone in a mushroom glade. In fact, between its howls it seems like it's whimpering.

"Do you think it's injured?" Mindy whispers.

"I don't know," Daz replies.

Oggie grips his axe. "Now would be the perfect time to attack it!"

Both the Tymbos tilt their heads. "Wait, friends! The Zarakna'rawr is not the creature we are seeing."

"Huh?" I say, confused.

"The creature we are seeing is what is known as the Oo'graw'nok."

"Oo'graw'nok?" Mindy ponders. "That can't be right. This is a gwarglebeast. The gwarglebeast is the Zarakna'rawr, isn't it?"

It is not. The Oo'graw'nok is this creature we are seeing. . . .

The almighty Zarakna'rawr is a creature we are NOT seeing.

"A deadly beast is the Oo'graw'nok . . . but much, much larger is the Zarakna'rawr," the Tymbos continue. "Being taller than the toadstool trees, with eight legs and eight eyes."

"Did you say taller than the trees?" blurts Oggie.

"Did you say EIGHT LEGS?" My hands start to sweat. "Is the Zarakna'rawr a SPIDER?!"

Mindy rubs her chin in contemplation. "I think something must have gotten lost in translation. We just *assumed* the mushrums were talking about the gwarglebeast when they said 'Zarakna'rawr.' But they were actually referring to another creature entirely!"

"Then what destroyed the railway?" I ask. "It was the gwarglebeast, wasn't it?"

"I'm not so sure," Daz says, staring at the creature. "Look at the size of it. It's not even all that big."

"You've got a point." Mindy refers to her notebook. "The book we read in the library said a full-grown gwarglebeast is about thirty feet tall. This one must be only half that size!"

"And look how it's whimpering," Daz says quietly.

Daz stands up abruptly and marches down the slope toward the gwarglebeast.

"Daz!" I hiss. "What are you doing?!" But all she does is put up a hand as she moves closer to the creature.

As Daz approaches, suddenly the gwarglebeast whips around, snarling ferociously. Daz recoils as the creature gnashes its teeth.

I draw my sword and charge. But Daz waves me off.

Daz takes a step forward, and the gwarglebeast shrinks back. I'm afraid the creature could bite at any moment, but Daz proves how great she is with animals.

"That's it," she soothes. "I'm not going to hurt you." She inches forward and places a hand on the gwarglebeast. It flinches, and so do I, but Daz is persistent. Reaching her hand out, she pets the monster like it's a puppy.

"Is she out of her mind?" Oggie whispers to me.

"No," I say. "She's *amazing.*"

"Well, what are you waiting for, everybody?" encourages Daz. "Pet him! It's okay."

"That was incredible, Daz!" Mindy beams as she pets the creature. "You've really got a way with animals."

"You, the one called Daz," begin the Tymbos, "rival the great mushrum beast-tamers of yore."

"Uh, thanks," Daz replies.

Oggie pats the creature's leathery back. "I guess he is kinda cute after all. What should we name him?"

I place my hand on the side of his head and scratch behind his little ear holes. He leans into my scratches, and then . . .

"Whoa, I think he likes you, Coop!" Oggie exclaims, and everyone bursts out laughing, even the Tymbos.

"Just my luck," I chuckle, drenched in slime. "But I think we may have stumbled on a name. . . . Slurpy!"

"'Slurpy' it is." Daz laughs and pets our new friend. "Aren't you a cute little Slurpy?"

"Wait, so if Slurpy is a baby gwarglebeast, then where's the mother?" Oggie wonders.

"That's a good question," says Mindy as she distractedly scratches Slurpy. "What if his mother was hurt or killed by the Zarakna'rawr? And now Slurpy is on the run?"

We're all pondering the possibilities when a distant, rumbling roar breaks the silence. Slurpy immediately cowers and starts to whimper again.

"Zarakna'rawr!" shout the Tymbos. "Zarakna'rawr!"

Another **ROOOOOAAAARRR** pierces the air, accompanied by earthshaking stomps.

"It's so loud!" I shout over the din. "Where's it coming from?"

"I don't know," yells Daz.

Before we can make heads or tails of anything, not fifty feet away the toadstool trees across from us creak and topple over with a massive **THUD!**

And then we see it. The largest monster I've ever laid eyes upon in my entire life.

And just my luck, it looks like a *spider*. . . .

CHAPTER

20

T HIS CAN'T BE HAPPENING," I SAY, PETRIFIED.
Of all the monsters in the world, Zarakna'rawr had
to be a spider! It's essentially the most terrifying
creature I could imagine. Huge? Check. Vicious? Check.
A behemoth of a fungus-encrusted SPIDER? That's a big
honking check!

Even as the shadow of the colossal spider creature looms
over me, I can't help but laugh. It's almost funny. Or maybe I'm
crying? Hard to tell, really, because the blood runs so cold in my
veins that I can't feel my body, and my feet are frozen in place.

In fact, I can't even move my eyelids. And I'd really like
to blink, you know? Because if I blink, maybe I'll wake up
from this horrendous arachnid nightmare!

BLINK. There! I did it. And . . . ?

Nope! This isn't a nightmare. There really IS a titanic mushroom spider monster, and it really is about to destroy us all.

"Look out, Coop!" Oggie tackles me just in time. Our bodies thud to the ground, and we roll clear of the spider's massive stomp.

"What are you—nuts?!" Oggie bellows at me, picking me up off the ground. "Run for it!"

Daz tosses one of her gemmed daggers into the air and catches it by the point between her fingers. With a swift spin, she hurls the dagger into the spider's leg.

The Zarakna'rawr lets out a bloodcurdling roar, unfazed by the dagger. As it stomps with all eight legs, its powerful footfalls shake the ground beneath us like an earthquake.

"Run!" Daz shouts. "Come on, Slurpy!"

Slurpy snarls ferociously, and the spines stand up on his scaly back.

"We are in agreement with the one called Daz." The Tymbos link their arms, one brandishing the shield, the other the spear. "We must be fleeing."

"There is nowhere to run, dungeoneers," says a voice.

That voice. *His* voice. The stranger who caved in the tunnel on us! From behind a tangle of webbed fungus, the stranger emerges, still hidden by the shroud of his hood. "I must say, I'm surprised you made it this far."

"You!" The words spill out of my mouth like icy water.

The stranger laughs, and above him the gigantic bulk of the Zarakna'rawr slows to a stop. Too many of its eyes blink at me hungrily.

"How are you doing that? How are you controlling the Zarakna'rawr?" Daz stares up at the creature in awe.

"Exiles can do lots of things."

For the first time I can see a wicked grin beneath the shadow of his cloaked hood.

"Exiles? Who is this guy?" Oggie asks with a waver in his voice.

The stranger throws back his hood, and his eyes blaze.

I can't believe my own eyes. I've only seen him once, just a tiny picture in the article we found in the library, but I'm sure it's him.

HA HA HA

"That's Dorian Ryder," I say.

"Dorian Ryder?" Daz and Mindy gasp in unison.

"No way . . . ," Oggie squeaks.

I step forward. "You were expelled from Dungeoneer Academy."

"That's right," snarls Ryder, glowering at me. "Being expelled from the academy was the best thing that ever happened to me."

"What?" Mindy says incredulously.

"Who are they to pick and choose who's worthy of being a dungeoneer? Who are they to throw away someone else's dream? You're all so stuck on that pointless Dungeoneer's Code! Blind to everything except your own backward ways!"

Ryder gestures with his glowing scepter. "Anyone can be an Exile. We're not wrapped up in dusty traditions. As long as you're tough, we won't turn anyone away. The Exiles are the future. Free to take what we want, when we want it."

"You're wrong!" I cry. "That's not what dungeoneering is about! You—you hurt your own classmates just to win."

"So what if I did? Dungeoneering is cutthroat. There are no RULES. Face it, we're treasure hunters, we're tomb raiders, we're destined to be the rulers of all these forgotten places that no one has ever seen. Weaklings have no place."

"No," I say, my voice steady. "We're explorers. Finders of lost things. Adventurers from every corner of Eem who come together to discover the magic of our world."

Ryder's eyes narrow. "What's your name, kid?"

I look to my friends and then back at Dorian Ryder. "Coop Cooperson," I say.

"Well, Coop . . . it's time to teach you and your little explorer friends a lesson." Ryder raises his hand, brandishing the scepter. "Behold! Thrall Wielder, Scepter of the Beast Queen Nylathar of the Shimmering Shar!"

"The who of the what?" Oggie peeps in my direction.

"Queen Nylathar. Founder of the first dweorg dynasty," says Mindy, deeply serious as she pushes up her glasses. "Legend says she used her magic to control the shadow beasts of the Impossible Abyss to conquer the Underlands. Really nasty."

"Shadow beasts of the Impossible Abyss? Great," Oggie says, his voice faltering.

Dorian chuckles. "You know your stuff. With this magic item I can command any beast to do my bidding!" Suddenly the Zarakna'rawr's eyes seem to spark to life, as if it were coming out of a trance. The scepter's glowing gem crackles and whirs as Dorian shouts, "Zarakna'rawr! Attack!"

The monster roars, its sound so loud and piercing that all I can hear next is a high-pitched ringing noise, and we all reel back in horror.

With reckless abandon we sprint away as the spider creature pursues us, its tremendous bulk crashing through the Fungal Jungle like an unstoppable juggernaut. With its enormous, scorpion-like tail it plucks toadstool trees from the ground and hurls them after us.

The only thing we can do is scramble into a nearby cave, barely escaping the monster's gnashing mandibles and grabbing palps.

"Hurry!" Daz cries as the Zarakna'rawr skitter-stomps after us. It's moving so fast that it can't slow down, and its momentum carries it hard into the cave wall.

We dart deeper into the cave as falling rocks and dust pelt us from above.

"Wait a minute," I say as my eyes adjust to the darkness. I can see now that the gloomy cave is thick with sickly mushrooms and a sticky, gray substance that almost looks like spider webbing. "Did we just run into the Zarakna'rawr's lair?!"

"I've got you right where I want you!" barks Ryder with sinister glee. He's walking casually, twirling his magic scepter behind the creature as it skulks toward us in the dark.

"Run! Head deeper into the cave!" Daz shouts, with Slurpy by her side.

"There's nowhere to hide! The Zarakna'rawr will do all the dirty work for me, just as I planned. . . ."

"Why are you doing this?!" I shout.

"Wouldn't you like to know," Ryder mocks. "But why would I reveal our plans to a bunch of little recruits?"

"Our plans?" I whisper to Oggie.

"Yeah well, at least we didn't get expelled!" Oggie jeers. "We're gonna be Junior Dungeoneers! And after that, we're gonna make it all the way to Explorer!"

"Shut up!" Ryder's tone turns serious and menacing. "I'm better than you. I'm better than ALL of you. See those

cocoons over there? That's the best Dungeoneer Academy had to offer. Pitiful."

I turn around and see a wall of what look like helpless people cocooned in gobs of sticky Zarakna'rawr web. It must be our entire class!

"Really? That's what this is? Revenge?" Daz scoffs. "Just 'cause you got kicked out of school?"

Dorian Ryder's head swivels like a viper as he tries to spot us in the darkness. "It's more than revenge!" he cries, voice thundering. "Dungeoneer Academy had its time. Now the Exiles are taking over. Under the leadership of our master,

we'll usher in a new generation of dungeoneers, the likes of which the Land of Eem has never seen."

"Master? What's this guy *blabbering* about?" Oggie grumbles with uncertainty.

"I don't know," I reply. "But we have to set the others free, or they'll be done for!"

"Help!" cries a familiar voice behind me. "Get me out of here!"

I run to the cocoons, each splattered against the wall like a spitball. One of them, hanging lower than the others, calls out in a muffled voice, "Help! Help!"

I slice a thick, gooey braid of the web with my rusty sword and pull Zeek out by his arm.

"You pinhead! You almost cut me!"

"A thank-you would have been nice," I mutter, helping a wobbly Zeek to his feet.

Dorian's voice echoes all around us. "Conversation time is over! It's the end of the line!"

"Look out!" Zeek yells. I swivel my head to see the Zarakna'rawr raising its forelimbs at Dorian Ryder's command, reeling back for a strike.

Zeek tackles me, and we roll clear of the four enormous legs crashing into the ground behind us. The strike is so powerful that the rock beneath us cracks like glass. Green Team scatters in all directions as the spider creature slams the earth again. Dorian's right about one thing. There's nowhere else to hide.

"Never split the party!" I yell to my friends, my voice quivering. "Stand your ground!" And to my surprise, they do stand their ground. Even Zeek. We all hold our ground together as a team and face down the monster.

The Zarakna'rawr opens its frothing jaws. Hot, musty breath whooshes over our faces, and with a calamitous bellow the spider beast sprays us with ropes of spittle and slime.

Daz dashes toward the creature's forelegs and strikes again before performing a somersault to dislodge her first dagger. "Go for the eyes!" she screams, and throws both her glittering gemstone blades at its clutch of glistening black orbs.

Oggie storms the beast's giant, twisted face and bears down on its head with his axe.

KA-KLANG!

Mindy flutters ten feet straight into the air and lets loose a crystal-tipped arrow that careens off the monster's thorax with a **TINK!**

Zeek winds up for the pitch and hurls a rock that crumbles off the chitinous armor like a clump of dirt.

The Tymbos link arms, spin toward the Zarakna'rawr, and smash their shield into its quivering mandibles, thrusting their spear into its mouth. **SHURK!**

I raise my rusty sword to strike, but the Zarakna'rawr's menacing eight-eyed gaze makes me hesitate. I get the sense that it can SEE my fear, and suddenly the sword feels heavy in my hands. I swing with all my might, but my weapon bounces wildly off its hard, armored carapace.

And then the monster swings back. I raise my sword to block, but the creature's powerful forelimb strikes so hard that the wind is knocked out of me. I slide across the floor wheezing, barely registering the monstrous shadow approaching. My ribs ache. My back throbs. The metallic taste of blood is in my mouth.

"Look out, Coop!" Oggie grabs my wrist and pulls me out of the way just in time.

Desperate for cover, we dive behind an outcrop of rocks and webbing to regroup. Every one of us is sweating, out of breath, and covered in nicks and scratches.

"What do we do?" Zeek looks at me with fright in his eyes. The others are beside him. I can see how scared they are, how utterly unsure.

"I wish that guy would just shut up already," Oggie pants. "Why don't we attack *him*?"

Daz wipes the sweat from her brow. "Even if we do and stop him from controlling the Zarakna'rawr, we're still gonna have to deal with that monster."

"It's no use!" cries Mindy. "The creature's exoskeleton is practically impenetrable!"

"It must have *some* kind of weakness," Zeek chimes in.

Scanning the creature's anatomy, Mindy points out the

fungal growth atop the Zarakna'rawr's head. "There! That might be its brain. Look how it's pulsating! That suggests there's no exoskeletal protection there!"

"*Might* be its brain?" Oggie flashes me a worried look.

Mindy nocks another arrow into her sparkling bow. "Only one way to find out for certain!"

"It's coming!" Zeek squeals, peeking over the rocks.

"We need a distraction!" I say.

We look at each other blankly. Then suddenly Slurpy arfs in reply, his giant tongue dangly and wet.

Slurpy bolts headlong into the open, heaving with every springy step. The Zarakna'rawr recoils as if surprised, and like two primordial titans, they snap and swat at each other, every blow a thunderclap.

Dorian Ryder dives clear of Slurpy's tail as it hammers the ground.

"Take the shot!" I cry to Mindy as the Zarakna'rawr's thunderous legs clamber toward us, tail whipping and mandibles chattering.

254

The Zarakna'rawr lets out a screech like a million—no, a *billion*—nails on a chalkboard. Its legs wobble and flail. Its eyes flash. Then, with the force of a mountain, the monster begins to fall.

Dorian Ryder scurries backward, feet pedaling to escape the toppling monster. But his foot catches a rock and he tumbles, dropping the magic scepter!

"No!" Ryder cries, snatching at the shattered pieces. "You fools! Without Thrall Wielder, I can't control . . . !"

The Zarakna'rawr scrambles to its feet, crashing into the surrounding rocks and knocking Ryder back down to the ground. It rears back to let out another monstrous roar, its fury unleashed, like it has just broken free from thousand-pound shackles. The Zarakna'rawr whirls its head to lock its eyes on Dorian, and the depths of its malice toward the Exile practically ooze from its mandibles.

"It's over, Ryder!" I shout.

Dorian seethes. "It's not over! It's just beginning! Our plan is already set in motion. You're all as good as dead!" Ryder springs to his feet and pulls a black gem from the folds of his coat. With a crackle of black light, a whirling magic portal suddenly opens behind him. "The Exiles will have their revenge!" he shouts with fury.

I can't believe what I'm seeing. "He's gone! He—he disappeared!"

The Zarakna'rawr reaches for the vanishing portal with its mighty claws. But the portal disappears in a blink of light. Clearly unsatisfied, the monster bellows in rage.

Mindy doesn't waste another moment and fires a second arrow at the monster's brain. But the Zarakna'rawr only gets angrier, all of its ire now focused on Mindy. Its monstrous girth crashes down toward her, and she's certain to be crushed if I don't help.

"Look out!" I cry. But I can't reach her! The monster's foot comes down hard.

But in the last second the beast suddenly jerks backward.

"Oggie?" I mutter, stunned by what I see.

With an amazing feat of strength, Oggie manages to hold the creature back, giving Mindy time to escape! But he can't hold on for long. With a whip-crack the Zarakna'rawr flings Oggie, who goes flying into the rocks.

"Oggie!" Daz cries out. Then, in spectacular fashion, she leaps onto Slurpy's back! Gripping tightly, she leads her monstrous mount on a death-defying climb up the cave wall, the gwarglebeast scaling the rocks with its powerful clawed feet.

The Zarakna'rawr thrusts its hooked stinger at Daz and Slurpy. They barely dodge the strike, the force of the blow cracking the cave wall.

"The joining of our efforts is what we must do! Distract the beast!" the Tymbos cry out, and hurl their spear at the Zarakna'rawr.

Zeek fires off another rock, this time connecting directly with one of the creature's eyes. The Zarakna'rawr growls, stomping in place as it turns its violent intent toward Zeek.

"Uh-oh." Zeek gulps.

"Look out!" I holler, and strike at the beast.

A wide-eyed Zeek slithers away behind a rock, where enormous threads of webbing snare him to the stone like an insect. "Coop!"

But before I can answer, the Zarakna'rawr swivels its chittering head directly at me, eyes glaring darkly. This time I'm overcome with fear, and my knees buckle. It's like I'm hanging from the vine in the Trial Gauntlet and Mr. Fang is staring back at me, looking right into my soul.

"Coop!" Mindy cries. "What are you doing? Attack it!"

I fumble my sword as I try to steady my shaking legs. The Zarakna'rawr turns its attention toward the Tymbos, swiping them away like rag dolls into the webby rocks.

My brain thinks, *Hey, you. Fang Face! Over here!* But no words come out. And I can only watch as Mindy aims her bow for another shot. But the raging monster flails, knocking her aside and sending her futile arrow into the ceiling.

Maybe Zeek was right all along. Maybe this unbelievable underground world of monsters and mazes just isn't meant for humans. Maybe I'm not meant to be a dungeoneer. Maybe I'm just another washout like Dorian Ryder! Well, minus the evil Exile part.

"Could use a hand, bud!" Oggie is battered and bruised but back on his feet, deflecting one of the creature's cruel, barbed forelimbs with his shield.

I know I've failed myself. And as much as that hurts? It hurts a lot more knowing I've failed my friends.

At that moment the shadow of the beast looms, eclipsing me in spidery darkness.

I raise my sword shakily, but before I can swing, the monster strikes. **FOOM!** The force is so great, I fly almost fifty feet into the air and tumble onto a stony precipice above.

For a second everything goes black.

"Coop!" Daz cries. I blink my dazed eyes and barely make out the blurry image of Daz and Slurpy leaping onto the Zarakna'rawr's back.

I'm shaky as I try to stand up, and when I blink again, I feel like I'm seeing double. Daz is now mere feet from striking as she bounds toward the Zarakna'rawr's pulsating mushroom brain.

"Come on, Daz!" I shout in a raspy voice. "You can do it!"

The Zarakna'rawr bats Daz and Slurpy to the ground, sending them spinning into Oggie, Mindy, and the Tymbos. I watch in horror as the spider shoots its web, splattering my friends, pinning them to the ground in cocoons, just like all the others.

At this point the situation is hopeless. We failed. I failed. Just like in the Trial Gauntlet . . . except this time . . . we're all going to *actually* die.

Just like when our sputter-car tumbled off the tracks, my life seems to flash before my eyes. Everything slows down, and I'm transported back in time.

I'm back home in River Country. I'm standing in the mud, a stick in my hand, watching my brother cry for help as a monstrous crawlbad rises from the muck.

I'm hanging from a vine in the Trial Gauntlet, Mr. Fang skittering below, reaching up at me from the darkness of the pit.

I'm back at Dungeoneer Academy, Zeek and Axel laughing at me as the rest of the class watches in silence.

I feel the sting of Zeek's punch bloody my nose.

I watch Tymbo nearly die at the hands of scumseers in that watery pit.

I see my best friends cocooned like bugs in a monstrous spiderweb.

I hear Dorian Ryder laughing wickedly as we face our doom.

I realize that all these moments are connected. They're like this big ball of feelings that are always challenging me deep down. I think about how far I've come, and how hard it's really been at Dungeoneer Academy. Never fitting in. Always being afraid. Worried I'll screw up. I think about everything my family gave up so I could have a chance at the life I wanted.

And finally I think about my friends. Daz, Oggie, Mindy, the Tymbos—heck, even Zeek. They're counting on me. The whole dang Mushrum Kingdom is counting on me!

My hand tightens around the handle of my rusty sword. I know I don't have much of a chance, but at least I have *some* chance. I have to try. A surge of energy floods my body as I peer down at the Zarakna'rawr hovering over my helpless companions. Then, as if sensing my defiance, the spidery horror turns its creaking, chittering head toward me. Its mandibles jitter wetly as saliva drools to the ground.

"Get away from my friends!" I command, and raise my rusty sword over my head.

And if I'm not mistaken, I hear the haunting rattle of what can only be the monster's hideous laughter.

"I'm not afraid of you!" I stand my ground as the Zarakna'rawr rises. Its powerful legs reach for the precipice with sinister intent.

Without hesitation I draw back my blade and make a running leap at the monster.

You heard that right. No more hesitation. We may never pass the Final Gauntlet or ever earn our Junior Dungeoneer Badges. But none of that matters now. Because whatever happens? I'm not going to let this overgrown arachnid hurt my friends. Giant spider monster or not, this is happening. Time to face my fears. After all . . .

DUNGEONEER'S CODE #10: FORTUNE FAVORS THE BOLD!

Suddenly, as I barrel down, sword in hand, a blue-green light floods the cavern. My rusty sword crackles and pops with energy, and in a flash of light the dingy blade transforms. The rust burns away, and the blade blazes with a blue-green flame, shimmering like a crystal.

The Zarakna'rawr's spider eyes light up with surprise as its mushroom brain twitches with confusion.

I cry out defiantly as I fall toward my enemy and strike!

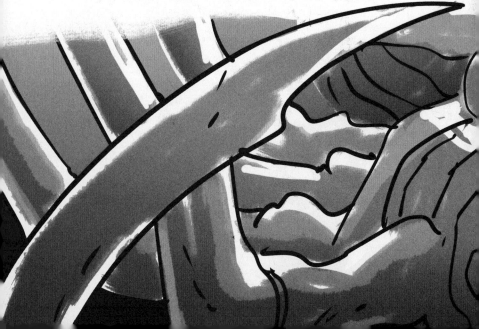

The Zarakna'rawr lets out a bloodcurdling shriek, and the cave shudders as the gigantic beast stumbles.

Blazing sword in hand, I spring from the monster's back to safety as it staggers one last time before all eight of its eyes go dark. Boulders crash and shatter as the Zarakna'rawr collapses to the ground, dead.

CHAPTER

I PICK MYSELF UP OFF THE GROUND AND USE
the light pulsing from the sword to search for my
friends. The chamber is filled with gloomy swirling
dust, and the shadow of the titanic spider, as dead as a
stone, looms over me.

"Hey! Are you all okay?" I call out, racing to a mound
of wriggling web cocoons. "I'm here! I've got you!"
SLICE! I cut through the gooey strands and knots.

Oggie and the others squirm free of the webs, clumsy
with excitement. "Coop! You did it!" Oggie exclaims, falling
over himself into a sticky tangle. "I can't believe it! HA HA!
You slayed the Zarakna'rawr!"

"It wasn't just him! We helped," Zeek mutters.

The Tymbos step forward timidly. "We are disbelieving
what our eyes clearly see. You, who are called 'Coop, Son of
Cooper,' slayer of Zarakna'rawr . . . you are wielding the sword
known as Crystal Blaze!"

Mindy whispers with awe, "The Crystal Blaze . . ."

"The Sword of a Hundred Heroes! The Sword of Mighty
Myko'morga'megalomungus, the ancient Mushrum King."
The Tymbos bend into a reverent bow. "You are favored by
the sword, Coop, Son of Cooper. For whensoever a cause is
being just and courage being true, the crystal blade shall blaze
with a flame that is righteous."

Suddenly I remember that the rest of our class and our professors are in need of rescuing from those gnarly cocoons! I slice a few open with a sizzling swipe. "Come on! We've got to cut everyone free!"

SLICE! SWIPE! SLICE!

"Ow!" Axel complains as he falls free and knocks his head. "Watch it, will ya!"

"Axel!" Zeek cries as he helps his buddy up. **SLICE!**

Arnie Popplemoose and the rest of the Blue Team spill out of the dangling webs, one on top of the other.

Another **SWIPE!**

Then the Yellow Team!

In a matter of moments the whole class is free. Professor Clementine, Coach Quag, Mr. Fang, and Headmaster Munchowzen all fumble clear of sticky knots of web and gunk. Everyone's dazed and uncertain of what's happened, like inside the cocoon they fell into a deep, unnatural sleep.

"Mr. Cooperson," Professor Clementine mutters, groggily adjusting her eye patch.

None of us reply immediately. Instead we just look to each other, like we're waiting for someone to take charge and explain things. But there's so much. Too much. At that point I smile at Daz, Oggie, and Mindy, and step forward.

"We're okay," I say.

Professor Clementine, still flush with confusion, replies, "Dorian Ryder . . . where is he?"

"He escaped," Daz says. "Disappeared through some kind of portal!"

"Escaped?" A grave look sweeps across Headmaster Munchowzen's wrinkled and weary face. "This does not bode well."

"Wait a minute," says Coach Quag incredulously. "You mean to tell me that you kids—the Green Team—defeated this . . . this giant spider creature?"

"The Zarakna'rawr," corrects Mindy.

It's just then that Headmaster Munchowzen seems to take note of the massive fallen monster behind us. "*Fungiformus tyrantula.* Known to the mushrum folk as the dreaded Zarakna'rawr! Why, such a beast is responsible for the destruction of the whole of the Mushrum Kingdom! Dorian Ryder took control of it! But it has been slain? How can this be?"

Before I can answer, Mr. Fang skitters forward. But I don't recoil in fear when I see him. Something's different. I'm not afraid anymore. And why should I be? Mr. Fang's the librarian. The only inkpot spider librarian in the world that I'm aware of . . . but hey, that's pretty cool. After all, I may not be the only human kid *ever* at Dungeoneer Academy, but I'm certainly the only one now. Mr. Fang and I are *wonderful onesies*, as my mom would say. So, in a way, it's kind of like we have something in common.

"Bless my stars!" Mr. Fang exclaims. "That sword you

wield, Mr. Cooperson . . . unless I'm mistaken . . . that is the legendary Crystal Blaze!"

The Tymbos step beside me. "You are not being mistaken. Coop, Son of Cooper, is wielding the Crystal Blaze, sword of Myko'morga'megalomungus, ruler of the Mushrum Kingdom."

Professor Clementine seems overcome with surprise. "Mushrum folk!"

"Well, I'll be!" shouts Coach Quag.

"This is incredible. No dungeoneer has made contact with the mushrums in decades." Mr. Fang offers two of his hairy legs to shake the Tymbos' hands. "It's a pleasure to make your acquaintance!"

"We are being pleased that you are not trying to eat us." The Tymbos shake Mr. Fang's outstretched spider legs.

"These are the Tymbos," says Oggie proudly, with an arm around each of them.

"It is an honor, truly," Headmaster Munchowzen says, stepping forward to shake their hands next. "On behalf of the faculty at Dungeoneer Academy, I give my deepest thanks."

"All the honor should be directed to Coop, Son of Cooper," the Tymbos say. "For he is being our king."

"Wait . . . what?" I barely get the words out before Professor Clementine jumps in.

"I'm sorry," she chortles. "Did you say Cooperson is your king?"

The Tymbos reply, "Whoever is wielding the Crystal Blaze is the one who is chosen by destiny—a hero being in a long line of legendary heroes. And also the rightful ruler of the Mushrum Kingdom, should they so choose."

"Coop, why don't you just give these mushrums their sword back?" Professor Clementine suggests.

I offer up the sword, but the Tymbos frown and shake their heads in unison. "Nay!"

Mr. Fang rubs his palps. "Hmm—then perhaps we shall put the sword in the academy vault, where it will remain safe and—"

"Nay!" the Tymbos say more loudly. "Impossible. Once the Crystal Blaze has chosen its wielder, the sword will be serving them for life."

"Wow," Oggie utters. "I guess my best friend's a king."

"Wait, so let me get this straight," I say. "You said I could *choose* to be the Mushrum King. But what happens if I say no?"

Because I still have a ton of school left, and, what with missing the Final Gauntlet and all . . .

I'm not even sure if I'll have the free time, y'know?

"We shall be honoring your choice, Coop, Son of Cooper. And now we will be returning to our home within the Mushroom Maze, where the legend of our adventures together will be shared. For your vow is now being fulfilled. Your name and the names of your valiant companions will be treasured amongst our people for generations."

"Uh . . . cool!" I say simply. Oggie, Daz, Mindy, and I all take turns hugging the Tymbos. They don't hug back, but they smile and let themselves be hugged.

"This is a moment of tremendous historical significance!" booms Headmaster Munchowzen. "After years of isolation, our cultures have finally come together." Munchowzen turns directly to me and nods. "Mr. Cooperson, you hold an artifact in your hands, a powerful relic that has been lost for ages, and carries with it a rich mythology and cultural importance. These mushrums wish for you to bear the Crystal Blaze, and

277

we will respect their wishes. As a dungeoneer in training, I hope you fully realize the responsibility!"

"I do, Headmaster Munchowzen," I say with a nod to the Tymbos. "I promise to take care of the Crystal Blaze and only use it for good."

"That is good!" the Tymbos harmonize as they nod. "And should you ever be needing the help of the mushrum folk, you will be knowing where to find us. Farewell, Team that is Green! We shall always be thinking of you as friends."

We exit the cavern and wave until the Tymbos disappear into the jungle, rays of light beaming down through the mushroom trees.

"Hey, Pooperson," Zeek calls out from behind me.

I turn and see that familiar, toothy grin, but somehow it's a little more friendly. "Yeah?"

"Listen. I just wanted to get a couple things straight between you and me." Zeek puts a hand on my shoulder. "We're never going to be friends, right?"

I'm about to stammer out a reply when Zeek interrupts, "But after today? Well, let's just say . . . you're not the worst human I've ever met."

"Thanks?" Wow, was that supposed to be a compliment? Considering everything that happened between us? Maybe this is progress?

Zeek sighs. "No, no. What I mean to say is . . ." He grasps for words, then repeats himself awkwardly. "What I mean to say is . . . I don't think you should get kicked outta Dungeoneer Academy. Not this year, anyway."

"I appreciate that, Zeek." I know that must have been hard for the guy.

Oggie sidles up beside me with a smirk. "So I guess you and Zeek are best friends now, huh?"

"I wouldn't put it that way," I say.

At that moment, bounding through the debris, Slurpy scrambles over to us, tongue wagging and giddy.

"Look out!" cries Coach Quag, who puts up his mitts. "Holy cow! A gwarglebeast! Defend yourselves!"

Professor Clementine and Mr. Fang bristle with fear.

"No, wait!" Daz steps forward. "This is Slurpy, our friend!"

At that, Slurpy licks profusely and whimpers with excitement.

"The gwarglebeast is . . . tame?" Professor Clementine marvels. "Remarkable. . . ."

Then Oggie chimes in. "We found him, lost in the Mushroom Maze, just like us."

"Can we keep him?" Mindy asks with a smile. "He's just a baby."

Headmaster Munchowzen approaches the gwarglebeast cautiously. "No, we can't keep him. These are rare creatures that live deep in the Underlands. Besides, this little fellow's parents must be worried sick." The headmaster places a gentle hand on its snout.

"Aw. But, Headmaster . . . ," Oggie protests.

Scratching the beast's chin, Daz smiles. "He's right, Oggie. Slurpy belongs in the wild. And if they're still out there somewhere, he belongs with his parents. We don't want to take that away from him." Her voice wavers a bit, and I know she's thinking about more than just Slurpy.

Professor Clementine leads us out of the Mushroom Maze, beneath the huge toadstool trees, and through the gardens of fungal blooms with their huge, colorful spores. At last we reach a rocky clearing at the edge of the Fungal Jungle.

"You're free now." Daz gestures. "Goodbye, Slurpy. Go be with your family."

22

THE LAST FEW DAYS BACK AT DUNGEONEER Academy have been a whirlwind. Everyone, including all our teachers, is amazed at what we were able to accomplish by ourselves in the wilderness. So much so that Headmaster Munchowzen has decided to hold a special award ceremony in our honor. And all of our families have been invited! Pretty awesome, right?

But there's one thing that's been bugging me ever since the Fungal Jungle. Where is Dorian Ryder? And who are the Exiles?

Right before the ceremony, I spot Headmaster Munchowzen in the hall, on the way to the auditorium. He's wearing a big green ceremonial gown and an emerald velvet fez.

"Sir, it's about Dorian Ryder," I say quietly.

"I see." Headmaster Munchowzen nods thoughtfully and gestures for us to start walking.

"There's something I haven't been able to wrap my head around, Headmaster. Dorian—he made it seem like he wasn't acting alone. Like there were more kids like him."

"You refer to the Exiles, yes?" The headmaster glances down at me as we turn a corner.

"Exactly. Do you know who they are?"

Munchowzen nods but doesn't speak. All I can hear is our footsteps. Then he starts up again, with a short sigh. "The Exiles are a group of former students. Students who . . . did not value the Dungeoneer's Code. They took risks, danger-ous risks. Didn't look out for each other. They were reckless and self-serving. Unfortunately, it seems they have strayed even further down a path of chaos and abandon."

"Lazlar Rake?" I wonder aloud. "Why does that name sound familiar?"

"Familiar indeed." Headmaster Munchowzen lets out a sorrowful sigh. "Rake was the cofounder of Dungeoneer Academy. We made many discoveries together. Lazlar was a former partner of mine, you see. But just as Dorian Ryder did, Lazlar lost his way many years ago."

"Before Dorian Ryder escaped, he said this was just the beginning . . . that the Exiles will have their revenge. . . ."

"It seems Lazlar will stop at nothing to destroy Dungeoneer Academy. Or perhaps even worse, turn our great institution into a training ground for thieves and tomb robbers. Unfortunately, he and the Exiles care little for understanding and preserving the past. They merely want to conquer the undiscovered world and claim its treasures for themselves. In fact, Lazlar became obsessed with one treasure in particular. . . ."

"What treasure was that?" I ask, enthralled.

Headmaster Munchowzen pinches his mustache nervously. "The stuff of myths and legends. An old relic. The lost shards of something called the Wishing Stone. Lazlar believed that if the shards could be reassembled, the magic power of the stone would grant him wishes."

"Wow. You mean you could wish for anything?"

"So the legends say." Munchowzen's bushy brow furrows.

"That's incredible!" I can hardly contain a smile, wondering what I'd wish for with a stone like that. Maybe every copy of *Dungeoneer Magazine*? Plus world peace and stuff.

"Perhaps. But in the hands of the wrong individual, a power like the Wishing Stone would be most dangerous. Some power is best left hidden and locked away from the cruel and greedy, like Lazlar Rake." Munchowzen absentmindedly fidgets with his gown. "He truly believes himself superior to everyone around him. And those Exiles of his are much the same—Lazlar has made sure of that."

286

Munchowzen shakes his head regretfully. "It truly pains my heart. There was a time, my boy, when Lazlar and I were friends. Now . . . those days are long behind us."

"Where's Lazlar Rake now? And the Exiles? I have so many questions!" I ask eagerly.

But Headmaster Munchowzen doesn't answer. He just smiles. "We should be on our way. It's time for the ceremony."

"I think he's talking about us," Oggie whispers, nudging me. And I can't help but crack a smile. I spot Zeek and Axel in the crowd, rolling their eyes and grimacing. I guess you just can't win with some people, huh?

"Unfortunately, all this commotion has postponed this semester's Final Gauntlets for the entire academy," Headmaster Munchowzen continues. "However, I can think of no greater test than what these four have already surmounted in the Fungal Jungle. And it is for this reason that I am awarding Oggram Twinkelbark, Mindisnarglfarfen Darkenheimer, Dazmina Delonia Dyn, and Coop Cooperson their Junior Dungeoneer Badges today."

I have to admit, I did NOT see this coming! We're officially Junior Dungeoneers! And we didn't even have to survive the Final Gauntlet.

The audience hoots and cheers for us. Well, except for two people . . .

"But that's not all," says the headmaster, quieting the crowd with his hands. "Not only did the Green Team demonstrate impressive bravery and skill in a live field situation, but they also exhibited true understanding and commitment to the Dungeoneer's Code, the Code that binds us all as dungeoneers.

"In fact, because of one student in particular—Coop Cooperson—we have decided to officially add an eleventh tenet to the Dungeoneer's Code: always do what is right, even if other options are easier."

"Whoa, you hear that, Coop?" Oggie exclaims.

I hear it, and I can't believe it!

"For in the face of danger, Coop Cooperson and the Green Team chose to do what was right, to aid those in need, despite enormous challenges. For this we are very proud." The headmaster looks right at us, a wide smile on his face.

"And so it is my great pleasure to award each member of the Green Team the Shane Shandar Badge of Dedication to the Dungeoneer's Code. A rare honor only ever awarded to a select few students at Dungeoneer Academy."

At this point the smile on my face must be from ear to ear. Headmaster Munchowzen pins both badges onto our sashes.

Everyone gives another round of applause for us, and we take a bow. Who would have guessed that we—the lowly Green Team—would ever receive such a high honor? I mean, just a few days ago we were fearing the worst about our futures

CLAP CLAP CLAP CLAP CLA

here at the academy. But now things are looking pretty bright.

When we get off the stage, all of our classmates congratulate us and give us high fives. (Well, except for you know who, of course.) I search for my family, but the auditorium is so crowded, I can't see them.

Instead two cloaked figures approach the four of us, their menacing red eyes shining from beneath their dark hoods. They look kinda creepy, like evil warlocks or something. My first instinct is to hightail it and walk in the other direction, but to my surprise, Mindy giddily runs toward them with outstretched arms.

"These are my friends, Mom and Dad!" Mindy says, pushing up her glasses.

"Hello, children," says Mindy's dad in a gravelly voice. "Any friends of Mindy's are friends of ours."

"Nice to meet you, Mr. and Mrs. Darkenheimer," I say. I guess Mindy's parents are more proof that you should never judge a book by its cover. They're not evil warlocks at all. They're nice warlocks!

Then I hear a booming voice, and at first I think it's Oggie because it sounds like the impression he does of his dad.

"Oggie! Oggie Twinkelbark!" A bugbear almost twice the size of Oggie strides up to us. He's so huge, he makes Oggie look like ME when I stand next to Oggie. Obviously, it's Oggie's dad, and he looks every bit the part of a mighty bugbear warrior.

"Hey, Dad," Oggie says a bit sheepishly. His demeanor seems to shift from the happy-go-lucky Oggie I know to someone a bit more reserved.

Mr. Twinkelbark slaps Oggie on the back. "Well done,

lad! Well done! I knew you'd make something of yourself if you just focused for once! I tell ya, I was pleased as punch to hear about the way you gave that big Zarakna-thing the old bugbear what for!"

"Thanks, Dad," Oggie says. "It wasn't just me, though. I want you to meet Mindy, Daz, and my best friend, Coop."

"Ah!" Mr. Twinkelbark gives me a friendly slap on the back that flings me a few feet. "A pleasure to meet you all!"

"Likewise, sir!" I reply.

"Now, I trust you've quit doodlin' all that nonsense in your notebooks, hm?" Mr. Twinkelbark says quietly to Oggie. "Better to do what us bugbears do best. And that's lifting stuff and walloping things!" Then his attention is caught by Oggie's shiny new gear. "Say, where'd you get this axe and shield, son? These are of fine make!"

"Oh, uh . . . we found the axe on our adventure, Dad. And the shield . . . well, I painted it myself."

"Huh . . ." Mr. Twinkelbark raises a skeptical eyebrow as he examines the shield in his hands. I can't tell if it's anger or something else that makes his mouth go agape when he says, "Painted it yourself, did you?"

"Y-yeah."

"My son painted this!" he shouts, startling Oggie. Then he turns to no one in particular. "Do you see this? My son painted this! Such craftsmanship! Such skill!"

"Hey, hold up, Oggie!"

"Yeah, Coop?"

"I just wanted to ask . . . You think you're gonna stick around? You know, stay at the academy?" I feel the words lump up in my throat. I'm not sure what Oggie's answer will be.

Oggie looks back at his dad and then to me with a smile. "Of course! After everything that's happened, I'm exactly where I want to be."

"Green Team forever?"

"Green Team forever!"

Just then I spot Kip, Chip, Flip, Candy, Tandy, Randy, Kate, Kat, Kit, Hoop, Hilda, Mike, Mick, and Mary, all running toward me, laughing and smiling. My mom is holding Donovan as she hollers, "There he is! There's the man of the hour!"

My mom straightens my hair and brushes the bangs out of my face. Then she gives me a wet kiss on the cheek. "Look at you. My wonderful onesie! Growing into a young man before our eyes."

My dad looks at me with that same quizzical look he had when I told him I wanted to become a dungeoneer. Then he nods, and his big bushy eyebrows soften. "It's not every day a dad gets to see his son become a hero. We're real proud of you, Coop." My dad tousles my hair with his big calloused hand, undoing my mom's straightening. "*I'm* real proud."

I turn around to introduce my friends, but I realize they've all gone their separate ways. Then I notice Daz off in the corner by herself. Just her and Peaches.

"Why is Dazmina all alone over there?" my mom asks me.

"I don't know. I guess her parents didn't make it to the ceremony."

The next thing I know, my mom waves Daz over like she's known her for years. "Dazmina! Dazmina, over here!" I can tell Daz is a bit surprised as she walks over.

"H-hi, Mrs. Cooperson," she says shyly.

"Daz, we've heard so much about you!" my mom gushes. "Coop just can't stop raving about you in his letters."

"Mom!" I say under my breath. I try not to blush, but I must look beet red by now.

"Well, it's true!" my mom says. Then she turns to Daz.

"Thank you for looking out for our Coop. Him being new and all. It gives us such peace of mind knowing he has friends like you around."

"You're welcome," Daz says. "And Coop's welcome too. I'd do anything for my friends."

My mom looks at Daz with soft eyes. I think her *mom senses* are telling her that Daz shouldn't be alone right now.

Before Daz can finish saying "Okay!" my brothers and sisters surround her and bombard her with questions. Daz shoots me a surprised glance and can't stop smiling.

"Hi, Daz! My name's Hilda!"

"Do you like Coop?"

"Can I pet your snagbunny?"

"Ooh, I like your hair!"

"How old are you?"

There's no saving her now. The Cooperson family has officially adopted her.

"All right, everybody!" my dad yells. "We're headed to Wally's Waffles and Weorgs! All you can eat!" He wrangles the group and heads for the door as my siblings cheer. Who doesn't love buttery, flaky waffles and crispy, juicy weorg drumsticks?

But before I join them, I take a minute to myself. Just a minute. With the assembly over, I'm the last one standing in the hall. I can't help but marvel at how I got here. Everything I've been through. Everything *we've* been through, me and my friends. Together.

This semester might be over for the four of us, but so much more lies ahead for me, Oggie, Daz, and Mindy. Sure, we might be screwups and we might not always see eye to eye. But we're a team. The Green Team! And for now Dungeoneer Academy is our home. Even if the Exiles show up again, we'll be ready for them.

Honestly? I can't wait to see what happens next.

After all, at Dungeoneer Academy . . .

. . . ADVENTURE is our favorite subject.

~ THE DUNGEONEER'S CODE ~

1. Discover new life and lost civilizations.
2. Explore uncharted places.
3. Unearth and preserve our collective history.
4. Expect the unexpected.
5. Never split the party.
6. Always check for traps.
7. Every problem has a solution.
8. Every dungeon has a secret door.
9. Cooler heads prevail.
10. Fortune favors the bold.

11. Always do what's right, even if other options are easier.

~ ACKNOWLEDGMENTS ~

We'd like to thank Kara Sargent, Dan Potash, Valerie Garfield, and the rest of our amazing team at Simon & Schuster that helped bring the book to life: Mike Rosamilia, Chelsea Morgan, Sara Berko, Alissa Nigro, Nadia Almahdi, Nicole Valdez, Anna Jarzab, and Michelle Leo and Christina Pecorale, along with their teams.

We'd also like to thank our awesome agent, Dan Lazar, whose sage advice helped Coop and his friends embark on their first adventure.

And, of course, a very special thanks goes to our loved ones, especially Kieu Nguyen and Heidi Chen, as well as Bug and Noodle.

Lastly, we can't forget our faithful Wizards of Eem on Patreon, whose support means the world to us: Amir Rao, Darren Korb, Elliot Block, George Higgins, Stephanie Beaulieu, Mercy Lienqueo, Daniel Madigan, and the Seventh Tavern.

~ ABOUT THE AUTHORS ~

BEN COSTA and JAMES PARKS are authors who have been friends since the second grade. In addition to Dungeoneer Adventures, they have created the graphic novel series Rickety Stitch and the Gelatinous Goo (for which Ben is also the artist) as well as the tabletop role-playing game Land of Eem.